Acting Edition

The Crumple Zone

by Buddy Thomas

ISBN 978-0-573-62767-5

www.concordtheatricals.com
www.concordtheatricals.co.uk

This work is published by Samuel French, an imprint of Concord Theatricals Corp.

MUSIC AND THIRD-PARTY MATERIALS USE NOTE

IMPORTANT BILLING AND CREDIT REQUIREMENTS

A New Comedy by
BUDDY THOMAS

Starring
MARIO CANTONE
with

JOSHUA BÍTON
STEVE MATEO

GERALD DOWNEY
PAUL PECORINO

Set Design
DAWN ROBYN PETRLIK

Costume Design
DAVID MILLS

Sound Design
LAURA GRACE BROWN

Lighting Design
ED McCARTHY

Choreography
PETER KAPETAN

Fight Consultant
B.H. BARRY

Production Stage Manager
GAIL EVE MALATESTA

Casting Director
PAUL DAVIS

Assistant Stage Manager
MICHAEL BIONDI

Technical Director
JEFF DUER

Advertising Representative
KELROM AGENCY

Press Representative
THE PETE SANDERS GROUP

Directed by
JASON MOORE

Actors appear courtesyof Actors Equity Association

Characters

TERRY   Late 20's — Early 30's.
A manic ball of energy with a scathing sense of humor.
Absolutely neurotic, with a tendency to hit the bottle.

BUCK   Late 20's — Early 30's.
Extreme GQ good looks, and just as charming. Love-
sick, and somewhat obsessive.

ALEX   Late 20's – · Ear'y 30's.
Constantly on the verge of a nervous breakdown, his
questionable choices get him into trouble.

ROGER   Early 30's — Mid 40's.
A big tank of a blue-collar man, sexy and dangerous.

MATT   Late 20's — Early 30's.
Boyishly good looking, somewhat naive and innocent.

Time

Not long ago.
Just before Christmas.

Place
An absolute dive of an apartment,
somewhere on Staten Island.

ACT I

Scene 1

(Almost 9:00 p.m.
The phone is ringing as lights rise.
The apartment is dimly lit, with only Christmas tree lights and the glow
of the television, which plays "How the Grinch Stole Christmas."
BUCK and TERRY lounge on the sofa, stringing popcorn, completely
ignoring the phone. The answering machine picks up.)

MACHINE. *(Voice of ALEX:)* Hi. Terry and Alex aren't here right now. Messages can also be left at this number for Matthew, who's on tour until April. *(Beep. Voice of MATT:)* Hey it's Matt. We just got here. Iowa. Iowa somewhere, some little potato patch from the depths of hell. We're supposed to be in Duluth, which at least has a traffic light, but the snow got so bad we had to stop —

BUCK. *(As message plays on:)* Okay, that's enough.

MATT's VOICE. — we're at The Blue Moon Motor Lodge, if you can believe it, um, 712 —

BUCK. That's it, turn it off Terry.

(TERRY turns it up.)

MATT's VOICE. *(Continued from before, no break:)* — 626-3484, room, hey, what's the room number...? Fifteen, room fifteen. Alex I really need to hear from you —

(BUCK has reached over TERRY and smashes down on the volume button. The voice ends.)

TERRY. What're you, nuts?!

BUCK. This guy calls ten times a day but I'm nuts.

TERRY. Buck, that answering machine is clingin' to life by a very thin thread, you don't need to be smackin' it and crackin' it every time you have some jealous titty attack, ughh, look at this, would you look at this?

BUCK. ... wha...?

TERRY. I hate the endings of Christmas specials.

BUCK. Why?

TERRY. They're always happy.

BUCK. Whadaya want, a homicide?

TERRY. I always resented the fact that the Grinch turns into this totally adorable, cuddly little pushover.

BUCK. ... 's'a kid's show.

TERRY. Great, so, so, why can't he, you know, steal Christmas, huh? It's called "How the Grinch Stole Christmas," let him steal the God-damned holiday and get off my TV screen!

BUCK. String your popcorn.

TERRY. I'm stringin', I'm stringin'... look at him! Laughin' it up with the dog! *(To the TV set:)* You're a villain! KILL SOMEONE!

BUCK. Bloodthirsty.

TERRY. I'm done, my fingers are tired.

BUCK. I bet you say that to all the boys.

TERRY. Only to you, Buck.

BUCK. What the hell is this? This is your string? Six pieces?

TERRY. LOOK at this ... that's it. I'm writing a letter to Dr. Seuss.

BUCK. You ate that entire bowl of popcorn?

TERRY. For psychologically warping the brain cells of every kid in America. This happily ever after stuff has gotta stop, I, I, mean, I want property stolen, and, and pets hit by garbage trucks, and little Whoville couples battling in divorce court, and, and I want Christmas stolen, just as is promised in the title!!! I'm sayin ... and incidentally, when Frosty melts, let him stay a PUDDLE! All this singin' and life is la, la, la, la, la, just, it's bound to set you up with expectations that can never come close to being met!

BUCK. What's wrong with you?

TERRY. I don't know, I don't know, life, I just, Christmas, I just-

BUCK. You just —

TERRY. I hate my life.

BUCK. You do not.

TERRY. Don't contradict me while I'm having a nervous break-down. I hate my life, I hate Staten Island, I hate the ferry, the landfill, this apartment, my job, what job, my Bachelors degree rottin' at the bottom of a stack of old *People* magazines, everyone famous but me, while I earn two bucks and very few tips an hour sloppin' pork chop platters around a diner that should've burned to the ground a hundred and fifty years ago, and, and, and, and —

BUCK. Relax.

TERRY. — and I just want that phone to ring, okay, once in a while, okay, for me, someone, anyone, phone sex, a serial killer, I don't care, and I don't mean Matthew either, fillin' up that answering machine all day, from Iowa or Omaha, wonderin' why Alex hasn't been writin' or callin' or —

BUCK. I don't know what you're goin' on about.

TERRY. Of course you don't, that's perfectly understandable, perfectly, your perfect face and body and your hair from the Final Net Hall of Fame, you've never been alone in the world —

BUCK. I've been alone plenty.

TERRY. Always a shoulder to lean on, never a desperate moment in a bar at three in the morning.

BUCK. Where's Alex, I thought he got off at eight ...

TERRY. Alex, Alex, Alex.

BUCK. He should be —

TERRY. So look at me.

BUCK. I mean —

TERRY. Look at me.

BUCK. Yeah, so?

TERRY. So .... so ..... what I was actually leading up to here, wondering about, um ... what do you think?

BUCK. What do I think?

TERRY. About me.

BUCK. Which personality are we referring to?

TERRY. Shut up, look, just ... just say it, basically, do I have a chance ever, at all, in any way, ever, the key word is ever —

BUCK. Ever.

TERRY. — of — taking our relationship beyond the friendship level, ummmmm, onto, a, you know, more intense level, just, ahh, feel free to smack me at any time before I make an even bigger fool of myself, and —

BUCK. Come on, Terry, you know the situation.

TERRY. I "know the situation." What, what is that? I "know the situation."

BUCK. I'm in love with Alex, Terry. You know the situation.

(TERRY has begun fooling around with the answering machine. Rewinding it, stopping it. During the following, he will press play several times.)

TERRY. Yeah, well how 'bout a situation where you're not gonna end up in a puddle of tears and Budweiser under a barstool.

(TERRY has pressed play:)

MATT's VOICE. *(Machine:)* — I really miss you Alex. Tonight I was looking at the stars and I thought —

(TERRY stops it. Rewinds some more.)

BUCK. You know how I feel.

TERRY. You know Alex is unavailable.

BUCK. Well, Terry, he's been pretty available, I hate to break the news —

TERRY. — as in attached, as in "happily ever after", as in married, as in hhhhh, it's disgusting, the more I think about it —

BUCK. Don't think about it.

TERRY. — the entire ... the whole ... don't think about it???

BUCK. Don't think about it.

TERRY. DON'T THINK ABOUT IT?!?!?

BUCK. Why are you getting hysterical??

TERRY. Hey. Hey. Hey. There has got to be —I know you're a little, um, infatuated —

(TERRY pushes 'play':)

MATT's VOICE. *(Machine:)* — don't return phone calls any more but I love you anyway —

(Terry stops it, rewinds some more.)

BUCK. Love.

TERRY. There's gotta be one microscopic moral squiggling around in your body somewhere! Some slight hint of guilt ... Anything ... ANYTHING??? Come on, speak, Buck. Prove to me YOU'RE NOT A MACY'S MANNEQUIN!!!

BUCK. You can't help who you fall in love with.

TERRY. Yeah, well too bad, baby, cause you fell in love with the most married man in the universe, and all the while, the vacancy sign in my bedroom window's been blinkin' like a neon light.

BUCK. I'd never be any good for you, Terry.

TERRY. I'd never be any good for you, Buck. My heart is as black as a coal. I'd be forced to cause you misery.

(TERRY presses 'play':)

MATT's VOICE. *(Machine:)* — love you Alex — *(Stops it.)*

BUCK. *(He's had it.)* Terry if you fuck with that again I'm gonna smash it over your head!

TERRY. Oh, nice, well, one more thing, then I'll never mention it again, I swear, I ...You're my friend, Buck. But so is Matthew. And so is Alex. And Alex will never ... ever ... leave Matt .... not even for someone as perfect as you.

BUCK. So what, okay?

TERRY. It's true.

BUCK. You don't know. You don't hear what Alex says to me.

TERRY. I don't wanna know, I don't wanna hear. God help me. I live in Knots Landing.

BUCK. Matthew's been on this tour for almost a year. Gone. Okay? How can you keep holdin' onto someone who's not even around to, to, you know, hold?

TERRY. What is that, your business?!

BUCK. Is any of this your business?

TERRY. It's my business, all right when my best friend calls me from God-damned Duluth at six in the morning and wants to know how his lover is doing, and I politely remember to forget that his lover is ten feet away in the other room with a cock in his mouth!!!

BUCK. Everything's about sex to you, right?

TERRY. You don't get it.

BUCK. No you don't get it, Terry. Stay out of it.

TERRY. Great. Great! That's just —

BUCK. — cause Terry —

TERRY. No, I'm OUT!

BUCK. — it's none of —

TERRY. — you're right!!! You're right!!! My life is pure soap opera and I'm not even a main character in it!!! I'm a supporting character in my own life!!! And you know what, Buck? That's just the way I like it!!! *(ALEX enters, wearing a Santa suit, a heavy jacket.)* Right, Alex?

ALEX. Right Terry, just don't start raving, my head'll pop.

BUCK. He's been raving for hours, his battery's gotta die soon —

TERRY. But I'm out of it, Alex.

ALEX. Out, great, just —

BUCK. Where ya been?

ALEX. Where've I been?

BUCK. You got off at eight.

ALEX. Buck, at eight o' clock, the line to my throne stretched half a mile through the mall. I felt like an attraction at Disney World.

TERRY. Only two shopping days left —

ALEX. — til the unemployment line, I gotta get outa this thing, it's like being buried in a big wool coffin.

(Through the following, ALEX is in and out of his bedroom, changing into a robe.)

BUCK. *(Unzips him:)* You smell like a toilet.

ALEX. Yeah? You bounce five hundred diapered asses on your

lap and see what happens.

TERRY. Still scarin' the shit out of em', I see.

BUCK. Come on Santa, come sit on my lap.

ALEX. Later, I gotta relax, I gotta just-

TERRY. Ya work tomorrow?

ALEX. Don't ask stupid questions, huh?

TERRY. The, Al, hey the national tour thing, the *Anything Goes* audition's tomorrow —

ALEX. — so whadaya want? You want me to pay the rent or you want me to get my ego destroyed for the ten thousandth time?

TERRY. You haven't been to an audition since October!

ALEX. Terry, when you can't even get hired for a Japanese industrial laundry detergent show, it sorta crushes any last remaining visions of your name in lights at the Helen Hayes.

TERRY. So what're you? Giving up?

ALEX. So what're you, my agent?

TERRY. Maybe I should be. You're going with me tomorrow. You can sing that thing from Carnival you always —

ALEX. Sorry, Pollyanna, the landlord waits for no one. And how'd you get outa work?

TERRY. I didn't.

ALEX. Good plan. Both of us as bag ladies'll be lots of fun.

TERRY. You're calling me in sick, and don't give me any shit about it cause —

ALEX. Call yourself in sick, I'll be over at the gingerbread hut, gettin' pissed on.

TERRY. Tell him, Buck. He listens to you. Your career is melting!!!

BUCK. Yeah, Al, actually, I was gonna talk to you, see, there's sort of a good position opening up in my office, it's —

ALEX. What fuckin' career, Terry?

TERRY. What?! No, hey, sorry —

ALEX. What position?

TERRY. Wait, hey, hello, it is time for Alex to learn the magical art of self sufficiency, okay, ever since he met you, he's had every job

the Staten Island mall has to offer.

BUCK. I got pull. I can't help?

TERRY. You've got *PULL*?! In the Staten Island MALL?!? This is something to be proud of?!?!? This is something to ADMIT?!?

ALEX. And I've got a mother already, Terry.

BUCK. Hey, just—

TERRY. Operator, inventory, SANTA CLAUS?!? Ya gonna play the Easter Bunny too?!

BUCK. Those were temp jobs, TEMP, this is a real position, a good position —

TERRY. There is *NO* good position at the Staten Island Mall!!!

ALEX. Serious...?

BUCK. — was gonna talk to you —

TERRY. Ughh.

BUCK. — guy's leavin' in the mall administrative office —

TERRY. That's your office, Buck.

BUCK. It's twenty-six five a year —

TERRY. His desk squeezed right up against yours, of course —

ALEX. Okay, enough.

TERRY. Maybe your destiny, Buck, is to wrinkle up and grow a goiter in the fluorescent haze of office light —

BUCK. You don't know what you're talking about.

TERRY. — Staten Island MALL office light for Christ sake, ugh, hey, this, THIS man is a man of talent, you never saw him act, you never saw him flyin' all over a stage with sweat and drool and angst spewin' outa his mouth —

BUCK. Sounds pretty.

TERRY. — throwin' himself against the walls, tearin' at his hair —

ALEX. Terry.

TERRY. I'm sayin', all I'm saying is that this man is one day gonna have about nine Academy Awards marching across his mantle, so I'll thank you for not dragging him down to your level.

ALEX. No one's draggin' anyone anywhere, Jesus Christ —

BUCK. And Terry. Get yourself a fuckin' life. You got your nose so far up everybody's ass, I'm surprised we can still hear your bitchin'.

TERRY. Yeah, well, the bitch is going to bed, so try to keep the moanin' and groanin' to a low roar tonight, huh, I need to not have black bags under my eyes for once —

ALEX. Terry!

TERRY. —and do NOT forget to call me in sick tomorrow —

ALEX. Sick with what?

TERRY. A heart attack. Cancer. Tuberculosis.

ALEX. Great.

TERRY. Better. A death in the family. My mother died.

ALEX. I refuse to tell them your mother died so you can go tap dance for the road tour of Anything Goes!!!

TERRY. Hellooo, it's a diner, not a worldwide corporation, death and disease are the only things these people understand, okay? What do they care if I drip snot all over the tuna melt deluxe, as long as their cash register is ringin', they could give a shit, so KILL my God-damned mother, she got hit by a garbage truck, her large intestine exploded, she jumped off the Statue of Liberty! I don't care! Just kill the old lady and let me audition in peace!

(He storms into his bedroom and slams the door.)

BUCK. Move in with me.

ALEX. Cut it out, Terry's great.

BUCK. Move in with me anyway.

ALEX. What's with this job?

BUCK. I'm serious.

ALEX. Twenty-what? Twenty-six somethin'? Pretty sad when that sounds like a gold mine.

BUCK. Listen, I wanna —

ALEX. Do I have to type?

BUCK. Al, shut up, huh, I'm serious. I wanna, I been wantin' to talk to you, it's the perfect way I wanna start the new year.

ALEX. What are you babbling about?

BUCK. By starting our lives together.

ALEX. Buck, it's been a rough day.

BUCK. I want you to move in with me.

ALEX. Let it go, huh?

BUCK. It's stupid. You live in this rat box, I'm always here, you're always there, it's —

ALEX. Not tonight, okay, I'm .... not in the mood. .... Didn't your mamma ever tell ya not to nag Santa Claus?

BUCK. *(Continues from above, no break:)* — it's stupid, Alex, all the money you waste on rent, you could —

BUCK. You're not listening to me!

ALEX. Look. I got stuff to figure out, I gotta go to bed and dream about blowin' up the North Pole.

BUCK. Wanna hear one of my dreams?

ALEX. I don't know, you're on a roll tonight.

BUCK. You. Me. A huge deserted beach. Ocean and sand forever. Just for us.... You. And me.... You gotta swim underwater through a cave to find it. Stars all over when ya get there. Moon makes the water like glitter.

ALEX. Ya had a few beers with Terry, didn't ya?

BUCK. You don't like my beach?

ALEX. I love your beach. Let's hit it. I gotta get outa here.

BUCK. So let's get out of here. That's another one of my dreams. You. Me. A road that doesn't end-

ALEX. Why, um, why do all these dreams begin with ... you ... me...?

BUCK. Why not?

ALEX. Cause, um —

BUCK. I'd do that, too. Get in a car and just drive. I always wanted to be going somewhere, anywhere, just away ... away from wherever I was. When I was a little kid, I used to get on the phone, middle of the night when everyone was asleep, call up every bus line, airline in the book. Make all these reservations to every single place I could think of. Hawaii, Alaska, South America, all these "exotic" places. New York ... tall buildings. Bright lights. Huh ... I was gonna save all my pennies, all my allowance until one day I could actually get on one of those big silver planes and fly right out of my sad little life, onto, into ... something ... anything else ... my great escape ...

huh. Look where I finally escaped to … Staten Island. Crazy, right? This is a place people escape FROM.

ALEX. Okay. Listen.

BUCK. I love you.

ALEX. *(As if he were slapped:)* Stop, sh—, j-what's the rush?!

BUCK. I —

ALEX. Huh? Just —

BUCK. What's wrong?

ALEX. Nothing! I dunno. Just —

BUCK. What?

ALEX. I've been thinking.

BUCK. Thinking.

ALEX. Yeah, and —

BUCK. See, everyone is always "thinking" around here. Hey. Come on. Don't think.

ALEX. Buck.

BUCK. Don't think. What's it do, huh? Gets your emotions all tangled up in a hundred knots and —

ALEX. Cut it out, fuck, all right?! I have something to say.

BUCK. Al. I know what you're gonna say.

ALEX. No you don't.

BUCK. You miss Matthew.

ALEX. Just stop.

BUCK. I mean a lot to you but this can't go on —

ALEX. Yeah, great, you've made the point —

BUCK. It can't go on, it can't go on …….. and then we kiss for an hour and rip each other's clothes off and —

ALEX. Fine. You've got me all figured out.

BUCK. I just thought I could save us some time and we could cut straight to the kiss.

(The phone starts ringing. They ignore it.)

ALEX. Look, we both need to think about how this got started —

BUCK. — shoulda thought of that five months ago —

ALEX. — the fact that if we actually thought about what we were doing, this never would've started in the first place!

(The answering machine picks up.)

MATT's VOICE. *(Machine:)* Hey it's me. Thought I'd try you one last time before I —

(ALEX has scrambled to the machine and turns the volume down as fast as he can. An awkward moment. BUCK stares at ALEX, furious.)

BUCK. Alex. Wake up. Regardless of your "thinking" and shit, it did get started.

ALEX. So what is that? Good?!

BUCK. Of course it's good! I love you!

ALEX. — throw that expression around like it's salad dressing! I've been with Matt four years! That all gets to crash to pieces now?!?

BUCK. It crashed the first time you flirted with me at the mall.

ALEX. Don't be an idiot, huh. I wasn't flirting, I was lost.

BUCK. You got that right.

ALEX. I just wanted directions, okay?

BUCK. To my bedroom?

ALEX. Forget it! I can't do this!

BUCK. The boy's been gone a year, Alex, face it! If it wasn't me, someone else woulda picked your ass up at the Orange Julius!

ALEX. I can't do this Buck! It's over!

BUCK. You're kidding, right? You gotta be kidding here. What have I asked you for?

ALEX. Oh, just to move in with you, nothing major.

BUCK. We have good times! You make me happy! That's more than enough for me!

ALEX. You said —

BUCK. Whatever, Alex, fine, ya know? You don't want me in your life, just say it. I been dumped before.

ALEX. If you have to hear the words —

BUCK. You bet I do.

ALEX. Then here they are.

BUCK. Drum roll, please.

ALEX. Buck ...

BUCK. ... Alex.

ALEX. I ..... love you ...

BUCK. Ooooohhh, that sounded painful, you need to go to the emergency room?

ALEX. *(Ignores him:)* Some — somehow it seems somewhere I fell — fallen — fell, in .... love — fu, you know, words, they're just words is all, no one knows what they mean, everyone just says 'em cause they hear 'em on the radio and on TV and at the movies and the whole world wants to be Julia Roberts and Richard Gere in the setting sun, love, it's just a word, okay, everyone says it so that makes it okay and —

BUCK. You're in love with me.

ALEX. Whatever it means, I don't know what that means. My heart always beats a little faster when I think you're about to walk into a room, and ... when I first see you ... I, um ... I get a feeling like a, a, a .... well ... and if I ever think you're in trouble or unhappy or something bad, um, I just, I mean, I don't know what I mean ... I, I know what I mean but I don't know how to, to —

BUCK. Alex. I know what you mean.

ALEX. I just mean that if that's what love is, then, yes. I'm very, I guess very much in love with you. But ...

BUCK. ... but. I'm still in love with Matt. And I've been in love with him for a long time, I'm sayin' for years, okay? He's deep inside my heart. I've only known you a few months and yeah, sure, things end, people change, but when you put a few months next to a few years, and, and the emotions invested and —

BUCK. Okay, fine.

ALEX. — and the —

BUCK. It's fine, forget it.

ALEX. I've only got one life. Not two.

BUCK. What did I just say? Did I say it was fine??

ALEX. It's sensible.

BUCK. Sensible, Alex? Now love is supposed to make sense?

ALEX. I'm sorry —

BUCK. Tell that to every single person who ever walked the face of the earth. Love is supposed to make sense. They'll laugh you right off the planet.

ALEX. I don't know what else to do, I don't know what —

BUCK. It's fine, Alex. It's fine. *(He goes to the door.)* Have a nice life. You and your sensible love. Flyin' around Jupiter and Saturn and all the stars in the Milky Way.

(BUCK smiles sadly at ALEX and exits, leaving the front door wide open. Alex stares after him a moment, shaky and lost. A moment passes and he goes to the answering machine. Rewinds a moment, then presses play.)

MATT's VOICE. *(Machine:)* — my phone bill at these hotels, but Alex, I just wanted to say, that, you know, whatever the reason is that you've been avoiding me, and you have been avoiding me, it's, it's, pretty obvious and all, but whatever the reason is ... I um, I still love you ... and just don't give up on me yet. This tour is almost over, and, okay, enough already. I just don't want you to forget about me ... okay? Okay. Annnnnnnnd ... to insure that you won't forget about me, I'm gonna run that answering machine tape right into the ground with a little schmaltzy selection dedicated especially to you. You're tuned to W.M.A.T., and this one goes out to Alex ... the love of my life ... with all my heat and soul ....

(Music begins. It is a sentimental Christmas song. As it starts to play, BUCK appears in the open doorway. Knocks on the door softly. ALEX turns, sees him. They stare at each other as the music continues to play. BUCK crosses into the apartment to ALEX. They stand very close. BUCK touches ALEX's face. ALEX hesitates, pushing his hand away. BUCK pauses a moment, and then turns to go, but ALEX pulls him back. They hesitate, and then, they kiss, softly at first, and then with great passion, as the music plays on, and the lights FADE TO BLACK.)

Scene 2

(The next day. Twilight.
There are several large and obnoxious bouquets of flowers on various
tables. The apartment is dark. The tree is off. Momentarily, a key
turns in the front door, and TERRY enters, home from his audi-
tion. Outside, it is pouring snow, and he is covered in it. He turns
on a light, throws his dance bag down, and ROGER enters, a big
tank of a man, a few years older than TERRY. He is just as ice-
covered.)

TERRY. What the hell's the matter with these people, they got
the heat set at like ten degrees —
ROGER. Seems okay —
TERRY. Shut the, come on, the, the door, it's the fuckin' Alas-
kan tundra out there, Christ, I'm gonna, I can't even —
ROGER. Cool tree.
TERRY. Huh? What?
ROGER. The —
TERRY. Oh, yeah, you know, I never knew snow fell horizon-
tally before, before today. Fell, right, more like blew, gusted, um,
whipped, smacked —
ROGER. Interesting words.
TERRY. Interesting day. What the fuck are all these flowers?!
Excuse me, I don't usually talk like I'm in a rap video, but snow turns
me into a raving foul-mouth pig!
ROGER. *(Moving toward him:)* Mmmmmm, sounds good to me.
TERRY. And, uh, I don't usually bring home strays —
ROGER. Strays?
TERRY. — so hang out over, sort of over there, in case you turn
out to be an axe murderer, I have time to jump out the window.
ROGER. My weapon of choice is the ice pick.
TERRY. Great, I'll see if we got one handy. *(He heads to the*
kitchen.) Whadaya drink? Do you drink?
ROGER. I —
TERRY. You live on Staten Island, of course you drink, I'll mix
you up somethin', I work wonders with fifty-nine cent vodka, what are

all these hideous flowers?!

(TERRY exits.)

    ROGER. They look like, aren't they like, those, uh, funeral, uh, you know, flowers, uh … you don't think someone died, do you?
    TERRY. *(Kitchen:)* Nobody died. Everyone I know is too bitchy and hateful to die.

(ROGER has been looking at the flowers … at a card.)

    ROGER. Aw, wow.
    TERRY. *(Kitchen:)* Yeah, I hope you like really, really, cheap vodka mixed with really, really cheap orange juice, I mean hey, the way I look at it, booze is booze, if it knocks you on your ass, it's done its job, right? And in a way, what more can you ask for?
    ROGER. Hey there, Tony, you maybe need to come out here a second —
    TERRY. Probably only alcoholics talk like this, but good. Fine. Great. Let me be an alcoholic. I, in fact, hope I am an alcoholic. My life is pure unadulterated hell, and now, Staten Island has turned into Siberia and my apartment has turned into daytime television, not the game shows, although a few people do seem to be after the same prize, not me, I don't mean me, nobody's after GOD-DAMNED ME in this apartment or this galaxy but I'm just saying, fuck it! I have no intention of dealing with these events sober, I have no intention of dealing with my life sober, and if that damns me to Hell with a pitchfork up my ass for eternity, then hot-damn hallelujah! That is just fine with me! Betty Ford, baby, here I come!

(He enters, two drinks.)

    ROGER. These um … seem to be, for, um … you.
    TERRY. Yeah? Someone finally sends me flowers and they're sympathy flowers? Who thinks I'm dead? My ex-lover. Oh wait. I forgot. I don't have an ex-lover!!! Silly me......You wanna be my ex-lover, Roger?

ROGER. No, um, some — someone else seems to have, uh, you know. Died. Uhhh, you better — uhhh —

(He thrusts the card at TERRY.)

TERRY. Yeah?... From my boss? *(Reads:)* "Dear Terrence, from all of us ... our deepest sympathies on the sudden passing of your ... MOTHER?!?

ROGER. *(Quickly:)* Aw, man, aw, I'm so sorry, what a way to, to find out, really, I should go, I —

TERRY. *(Finally, annoyed realization:)* Awwwwwww .... fuck. Ju — great. Just great.

ROGER. Um ... what?

TERRY. Great. Unbelievable. Do you know what it's like to live with a roommate, a brain the size of a turnip seed?!

ROGER. But —

TERRY. I mean what do they think, huh, what —

ROGER. — wait, your, your mom-mother's dead, and —

TERRY. — she's not dead —

ROGER. But —

TERRY. She's alive and kickin' but I'll give these to my room-mate after I kill him.

ROGER. I don't get it.

TERRY. This audition today, this waste of good oxygen today, I'm scheduled to work, right, you follow me? So I jokingly, jokingly, the key word here is jokingly, okay, I jokingly say to my roommate, Alex, I say, "Alex, please call me in sick today", and here comes the jokingly part, get ready, I say "make it serious", that's not the jokingly part, it had to be serious because my boss is the Anti-Christ, but Alex doesn't get it, doesn't know what to say, so, here comes the jokingly part, pay attention, I jokingly say for him to call me in sick by saying that my mother died. Jokingly.

ROGER. So you, umm, you didn't want him to call you in sick?

TERRY. Um, am I speaking in a strange Creole language here? He could've said the flu, he could've said, I dunno, I fell down a flight of stairs, instead he says my mother died.

ROGER. But you told him to, I, I don't get it —

TERRY. Not to mention the fact that he probably put a curse on the old lady, she's prob'ly fallin' down a manhole even as we speak. This is great.

ROGER. It's sick.

TERRY. You got that right. Now I gotta take days off to mourn, to view the body, do the funeral, I mean I'm sayin', I got bills due, rent, the landlord don't wait for imaginary funeral processions!

(ROGER has taken a drink. He nearly gags.)

ROGER. Jesus, what is this, Clorox???

TERRY. I like my drinks the way I like my men. Strong and cheap.

ROGER. Jesus Christ.

TERRY. Aw, lighten up, I don't really. I just like to say that line.

ROGER. Are you sure you're not on some kind of special release program from the mental ward?

TERRY. Yeah, well, I gotta be crazy to live in this hellhole, spend forty, fifty hours a week runnin' around with fried eggs and French fries in my hands, an extra twenty hours draggin' out to these auditions, hopelessly, hopelessly hoping that one of these times, they might actually look up from their bagel and coffee and watch me sing! "Thank you, NEXT!!!" I gotta be crazy. With a Bachelors degree. A forty-thousand dollar fucking Bachelors degree!!! Do you have a Bachelors degree???

ROGER. No, um, but, uh, I got my G.E.D.

TERRY. Yeah? You make a living?

ROGER. I, uh, manage a factory outlet for —

TERRY. Perfect, that's really the best! I go to college four years, sign my life away to the student loan companies of America, ruin my credit, all chances I'll ever own a car, a house, a plane ticket, slave until I'm dead in a grease hut, perfect! You drop out of school in kindergarten, prob'ly, and you're in management! WHO MAKES THESE RULES?!?!?

ROGER. Why, uh, why —

TERRY. Crazy, sure I'm crazy! Staten Island?! Be SANE and live on Staten Island?! With the fumes from the landfill seeping into your brain cells and turning them every color of the rainbow, the toxic air mutating your body step by step by step so that by the time you're forty, you look like a car accident! Me, sane? Please don't make me laugh.

ROGER. I like the way you talk.

TERRY. That means you're pretty screwed up too, fella.

ROGER. I think you're cute.

TERRY. Yeah, sure, ahhh, so … soo … um, what, you live on Staten Island, right, I mean you must, you were on the ferry, you, huh, stupid question, huh … um … you work here?

ROGER. Manhattan.

TERRY. Yeah? Where?

ROGER. Suddenly, I'm on the Barbara Walters interview.

TERRY. Well all I know about you is you like the window seat on the ferry, what do you want me to do?

ROGER. What do I want you to do?

TERRY. Yeah.

ROGER. Dangerous question.

TERRY. Not so dangerous. I'll do anything.

ROGER. Anything?

TERRY. Anything safe. Anything totally and completely and without a shadow of a doubt safe, which I guess means nothing. My life is a living hell, true, but the masochistic side of me intends to drag it out at least until I'm eligible for senior citizen discounts.

ROGER. You have a masochistic side?

TERRY. Why, do you have a sadistic side, is that what we're getting at here, Roger?

ROGER. I don't know.

TERRY. You don't know??? Well, whatever, just keep it hidden there Roger, the last thing I need is a body cast.

ROGER. I was just —

TERRY. Roger. Roger? This is actually your name or did you just make it up? Nobody is named Roger, Roger.

ROGER. I am.

TERRY. What's your last name?

ROGER. You ask a lot of questions.

TERRY. Yeah, so?

ROGER. So are you with the F.B.I.?

TERRY. Are you on the run from the F.B.I.?

ROGER. Are you gonna kiss me or do I have to get sadistic?

TERRY. I'm not kissin' a guy won't even tell me his last name.

ROGER. What difference does it make?

TERRY. I don't do one night stands.

ROGER. Maybe it won't be a one night stand.

TERRY. Maybe it will be.

ROGER. Maybe New York City's gonna crash into the ocean in fifteen minutes.

TERRY. Don't get my hopes up.

(ROGER kisses him. Long. TERRY does not resist.)

ROGER. *(Mid-kiss:)* Ramone.

TERRY. ... huh...?

ROGER. — my last name —

TERRY. ... oh ... good stage name ... Roger Ramone ... you sound like an action hero ...

(They are kissing urgently through the following, and ROGER is ripping TERRY's clothes off like he's opening a present.)

ROGER. ... action hero, huh? *(He peels his shirt off.)* ... more like the psycho bad guy, makin' love to you and kickin' your ass all at the same time ...

TERRY. *(In a sexual trance, but clicking out of it, slightly:)* ... sounds, um, rough ...

ROGER. ... yeah, you like that, Joey?... You like rough guys?

TERRY. Um ... Joey?

ROGER. You like that chest, you ever been with a guy as big as me?

TERRY. *(Snapping out of it now:)* Oookay, I'm thinkin', I'm kind of thinkin' maybe we should —

ROGER. Shhhh, you talk too much, why don't you show me what else you can do with that mouth ...

(He slams TERRY's head onto his nipple.)

TERRY. *(Tries to object:)* — b — I — ju —

ROGER. ... yeahh, that's it, just suck on that, give you a preview of comin' attractions.... *(ROGER picks TERRY up and carries him over to the couch like a sack of potatoes.)* Yeah, that's it, boy ... worship that body....

TERRY. I'm worshipping, I'm worshipping. *(This is too much. TERRY has been stripped down to nothing but underwear and ROGER is about to get rid of this too. Just as his head is about to make contact with ROGER's open zipper, TERRY struggles wildly up:)* Wait a minute, what do I look like, Marilyn Chambers?!?

ROGER. *(Grabs TERRY, pulls him easily down:)* You know you want it, you know you gotta have it, Joey —

(TERRY is basically face down in ROGER's lap at this point. ROGER pulls down the back of TERRY's underwear.)

TERRY. *(Struggling like a hooked fish:)* Who the fuck is Joey?!?

(ROGER slaps TERRY's ass hard enough to burn. As TERRY is about to react, the front door flies open and BUCK bursts in, just back from work ... sharp clothes, suit and tie, slightly hysterical, and freezing. Startled at the interruption, ROGER stands up, sending TERRY sprawling off his lap and onto the floor.)

BUCK. *(As he enters:)* Freezing, Jesus, God, it's like — *(Stops. Sees ROGER. Confused:)* Oh, uh. Hey.

ROGER. *(Instant attraction to BUCK. Forgets TERRY ever existed:)* Hey. Howsit goin' man?

(TERRY pops up from the floor like a jack in the box.)

BUCK. *(Baffled; to TERRY:)* What are you doing?

(TERRY has been scrambling to throw on whatever clothes he can find, but he can't find much. He has put it on anyway: a scarf, a coat, a boot, etc. He looks ridiculous.)

TERRY. *(Pure ice:)* He's not here. Get out.

(BUCK brushes past ROGER as if he weren't even there.)

BUCK. Terry. I gotta talk to you. I mean now.

TERRY. Excuse me? Wait, excuse me, what am I hearing?

BUCK. I'm goin' crazy here, you don't understand.

TERRY. Yeah, well I'm not your guidance counselor, and this ain't the time for —

ROGER. *(Goes over to BUCK, hand out:)* Howsit goin', man? Name's Roger.

TERRY. Heel, Roger, heel! He may be good looking, but his brain couldn't power an electric juicer.

BUCK. I gotta talk to you.

TERRY. I. AM. BUSY.

BUCK. He hasn't called me all day long.

TERRY. He's had toddlers on his lap all day long!!!

BUCK. He always calls, stops by, we go to lunch, he calls, I think it's over, Terry, fuck, I really do, last night we had this big blow out, you heard —

TERRY. Yeah, thanks for the black bags, bitch!

BUCK. — and then sure, it was bad, real bad, but I couldn't leave it like that, I couldn't, I came back, we kissed, went to bed, but he was cold or distant or somethin', shit, Terry, I don't know what he's thinkin'. I don't know what to do.

TERRY. So I'm supposed to know.

BUCK. Cause —

TERRY. Great, I'll tell you what to do. Go rent Fatal Attraction and play it fifteen times, full blast, cause Glenn Close had the same look in her eyes that I'm seein' now, AND I DON'T THINK I'M READY TO DEAL WITH BARNYARD ANIMALS FRYIN' IN MY SPAGHETTI POT!!!

BUCK. I need somethin' to drink —

(BUCK heads to the kitchen.)

TERRY. *(Chasing him:)* No ya don't, Buck, cause you're not staying!!!

ROGER. Buck? Your name is Buck? Cool, man. I'm Roger. Get

it? Buck? Roger? Buck Rogers??

TERRY. Holy shit, I think we just had a meeting of the minds.

ROGER. You live around here?

TERRY. That's okay, Roger Ramone. Flirt away. I'm not insulted.

ROGER. Cool.

TERRY. Cool. Um, actually, I think, let's call it a night, huh?

ROGER. You, um, want me to go?

TERRY. I gotta put on my Dear Abbey dress. It ain't pretty.

ROGER. Well, uh, Buck, it's nice meeting you man, maybe we could —

TERRY. No you couldn't. *(Opens front door:)* Merry Christmas.

ROGER. I mean if you'd want —

TERRY. Happy New Year.

ROGER. *(Hands a card to BUCK.)* — my card, s'got my beeper number on it —

TERRY. *(Swipes the card)* That's sweet Roger, two men an hour, is it hard being shallow as a puddle?

ROGER. Call me.

(SLAM! He is gone. TERRY collapses against the door. Glares at BUCK.)

TERRY. *(Tearing the card into a zillion pieces:)* Never. Ever. Ever. Come here again.

BUCK. Where the hell'd ya meet that one?

TERRY. The Staten Island Ferry. He was reading *The Village Voice* Men Seeking Men. He had a tie and a briefcase and a bottle of Bud.

BUCK. Love at first sight.

TERRY. Huh.

BUCK. Hey, thank me. He was a scumbag.

TERRY. Buck, I have not had a kiss in two years! At this point, I'd fuck Don Rickles!

BUCK. Look, I can't even —

TERRY. Quiet!

BUCK. — function or —

TERRY. Function your way out that door, how bout it?! The Staten Island Ferry?!? I picked up a man off the STATEN ISLAND FERRY?!? This is what my life has sunk to?!?!?!?!

BUCK. Big shit, Terry, at least you're not in love with —

TERRY. What?! Love?!? Fuck love!!!

BUCK. Ughhh …

TERRY. You can have any one you WANT, get it?!? LOOK AT YOU! G.Q.! Ken Doll! You're perfect, even with dirty snow in your hair!!!

BUCK. I want —

TERRY. You can have any one! What does that feel like, what about me, huh? What future do I have, ever, of finding anything slightly resembling happily ever after when the only men who want me are a very small handful of seventy-five year old pedophiles!!!

BUCK. You don't get it.

TERRY. Buck, you knew he was seein' someone, okay, you knew he was married, I have absolutely no sympathy for you!

BUCK. Fine.

TERRY. You knew it was serious.

BUCK. Huh.

TERRY. You knew they were —

BUCK. — so God-damned serious, how come he's been sleepin with me???

TERRY. Let it drop! Let it die, can you?! They are in love!

BUCK. And so am I.

TERRY. You're in love with Santa Claus, great. Is he in love with you?

BUCK. He said —

TERRY. Did he bake ya a chicken yet?

BUCK. What?!

TERRY. Flowers? A teddy bear? You got a stuffed animal, right, Buck?

BUCK . Give me a break, huh —

TERRY. No, I won't give you a break, Buck, cause I've known that corny queen a long, long time, and lemme tell ya somethin! It ain't love til he gives you a big fat teddy!

BUCK. Yeah but —

TERRY. Love, LOVE, LOVE, Jesus Christ, find me some gasoline, I'm goin' to burn down a Hallmark Shop!!!

BUCK. You can't help who you fall in love with, Terry

TERRY. Buck, it's garbage. You've known him a couple a months! You don't love someone you know a couple a months cause you don't even know them! And the only thing, actual concrete fact that you DO know about him is that he's been cheating on his lover of four years! Is this someone you wanna love?!

BUCK. Yes!!! No!!! I don't know, okay, I don't know what else to call it.

TERRY. Lust

BUCK. No.

TERRY. Stupidity.

BUCK. Ughhhhhh ......

TERRY. Bullshit.

BUCK. Terry —

TERRY. Take your pick, all answers are correct, here, drink this, it makes the world look like a Christmas tree. *(BUCK takes a drink. Then another. Then he drains the glass.)* Well ...... that's one way to do it.

BUCK. If I just knew what he was thinking —

TERRY. Stop it, I'm gonna drop razor blades in your cocktail, just, no more, I can't —

BUCK. Fine, fine, no more.

TERRY. It's a new year, comin', okay, a new start, we'll go out, you and me. I'm a great date.

BUCK. — just start over, let's do it, I'm a grown man, I got pride —

TERRY. Exactly.

BUCK. Self respect —

TERRY. It's a date.

BUCK. I can have anyone, who needs him, there's —

TERRY. You're starting up again. You're getting wound up.

(The front door opens, and ALEX enters, wearing his Santa suit and a heavy coat. He holds a bag, and a large wrapped Christmas gift.)

ALEX. Terry, I tell you to keep this door locked, one day when some kid flies in with a machine gun maybe you'll learn —

TERRY. Gee whiz, Dad, am I grounded?

ALEX. I don't need your fucking sarcasm tonight, just keep the door locked.

TERRY. Ohh, good, good, I'm actually glad you've decided to jump down my throat, cause now I won't feel guilty about jumping down yours —

ALEX. I'm not in the mood for —

TERRY. You told them my MOTHER DIED?!?!?!?!

ALEX. Ohhhhhhhhhhhhhh, do not even, even go there.

TERRY. Look at this! They sent flowers, the whole deal!!! This thing belongs on a drag queen's head!!

ALEX. Great, you can wear it out tomorrow night.

TERRY. Unbelievable, you got the sense of a —

ALEX. Buck, did this insane stump not stand RIGHT there in that doorway and order me. ORDER me to say his mother died, did, did, did this not happen, did —

TERRY. A joke!

ALEX. — right —

TERRY. Sarcasm!

ALEX. Terry. You need help.

TERRY. Yeah, well, I'll need help with the rent when they give me a week off to grieve!

ALEX. You stood right there and said they never give you time off because they're evil and Satanic and —

TERRY. They're Mafia, okay?! They sent flowers, okay?! Death and dying they understand very well!!!

ALEX. You, you, you just need therapy, and electroshock and tranquilizers and —

TERRY. So do you, your face is purple, you look like an Oompa Loompa.

BUCK. — enough —

TERRY. What are you doing home early anyway?

ALEX. I can't be home early?

TERRY. You're never home early, you're only home late —

ALEX. Well, Terry, guess what? I'm home early.

TERRY. You quit?

ALEX. I didn't quit!

TERRY. You got fired?

ALEX. What the fuck is it with you?! You're on my back twenty four hours a day, like-like-like some bird, j-p-pickin' at every open wound, every —

TERRY. You got fired.

ALEX. Terry!

TERRY. Cause if you did —

ALEX. I didn't get fired, Terry, I didn't get fired, all right, I just got .... uhmm .... fired. Okay. I got fired, fine, great, so what no one's ever been fired before? Does that make you wanna fly to Disneyland, somethin? They fired me, who frigging fucking cares.

BUCK. They can't do that!

ALEX. Forget it —

BUCK. I'm callin' Dave Hansen right now, this is bullshit, you were great with those kids ——

ALEX. Don't bother, few days, I'd be outa work anyway —

TERRY. Does this mean the Easter Bunny's out of the question?

ALEX. Well yes, Terry, I guess you're right again, whadaya know —

BUCK. What happened, what, uh —

ALEX. Nothing, stupid, just — I don't wanna talk about it — (They stare at him.) — these four little girls started telling me I'm not the real Santa Claus.

(He stops.)

TERRY. .... you're NOT the real Santa Claus.

ALEX. Well, I could be! I could be the real Santa, Terry! If you're five years old, if you still own a lunch box —

TERRY. — if you've got gumdrops in your head instead of eye-balls.

ALEX. I'm sayin' no one else had a problem with it Terry. All the rest of the kids believed, what was so different about these little bitches, look I don't wanna talk about it ——

TERRY. Well you're gonna talk about it, get him a drink, Buck —

ALEX. I don't need a drink, okay, the last thing I need is —

BUCK. You're fired cause some kid didn't think you were real?

ALEX. Not some kid, Buck. Four kids, four girls, sisters, okay?
Ugly little albino sisters with kinky red hair and paper thin skin, and
rich, they had to be rich, they all had matching dresses and all this
gold jewelry, these little girls, I'm sayin —

TERRY. You're sayin' they had power? They marched to the
White House and demanded your resignation?

ALEX. No Terry, I'm saying they were taunting me, telling me to
get lost, to drop dead, that I'm not the real Santa, and so I say, "Ho-
ho-ho, little girls, in fact, I AM the real Santa, and Santa does not
think this is very ladylike behavior." And you know what they said to
that, the little one I mean, the littlest one, she had to be all of four
years old, you know what she said to Santa, Terry?? To Santa Claus,
you know what she said? She said .... "Fuck you, cupcake."

TERRY. She did not.

ALEX. Yes she did, Terry, yes she did, and you know what she
did next?

TERRY. Ummmmm, lit up a cigarette and stabbed it in your eye-
ball?

ALEX. Well, I'm sure she would've if she had a pack handy, but
she didn't so she decided instead to spit on me and punch me in the
stomach and rip my beard off and run across the mall to the Gap, waving my beard in the air, and luckily, this Gap sales lady sees the whole
thing and she grabs it, you know, the beard, and runs back over to the
gingerbread house with it, which makes the evil albino girl burst into
screaming sobbing tears til all the Gap employees are rushing out to
see what the hell is going on, and what's going on is that right at that
exact moment, this cutest little kid in the world, five or six years old,
little freckles on his nose, little blue cap, little front tooth missing, he
comes racing up, and I'm trying to get my knotty, tangled beard back
on but the kid doesn't care, he thinks Santa's just havin a bad hair
day. He jumps right on my lap. This kid believed. All of a sudden, his
mother comes clacking up in her Payless pumps and her feathered,
Frost n' Glow poof-do that hadn't changed a LICK since she got
fucked on a beer keg at a frat party in 1985! She grabs my ear in a
Lee-Press-On fist and says, "Don't you DARE say you'll bring him a

doll!"... and she clacks away and stands there like a vulture, Virginia Slim hangin' outa her mouth, kid is totally oblivious to it. Just sits there smilin', bouncin' on my lap. Staten Island Mommie Dearest, blowin' smoke rings in my face. *(Takes a big breath, composes himself:)* The kid is there and I say, "Ho-ho-ho, little boy, what would you like for Christmas?" And-okay-ready? What do you think he asks for???

TERRY. ... a doll ...

ALEX. *(Pushes TERRY off:)* NOT just any doll, gentlemen, this kid has class.... He wants Super Sparkle Barbie Dream Date Deluxe.

BUCK. — oh wow —

ALEX. — and Skipper too.

BUCK. — wh, what did you tell him?

ALEX. What could I tell him? I tell him wouldn't he have more fun with a couple of G.I. Joes?

TERRY. God knows I would.

ALEX. Not this kid, nooooooo, he wants the one with the pretty dress. So you know what I say? Hey, what else could I say?

(They stare at him.)

BUCK. What did you say?!?

ALEX. I say "G.I. Joe looks good in a pretty dress too."

TERRY. You did not.

ALEX. Swear to God. Mommie Dearest hears me of course and yanks the kid off my lap so fast she almost knocks over the ginger-bread house, but wait! It gets better! At that exact moment, the mother of the evil albino sisters comes racing over, and the littlest albino is still wailing away and then both the mothers start screaming, SCREAMING, one cause I made her little brat cry and the other cause I tried to morally corrupt her son!!! And the next thing I know all the other parents are getting in on it and the Salvation Army lady drops her bell on the floor and runs over and starts screaming that I'm gonna burn in hell for ruining Christmas, and every child in line bursts into tears and the four evil albinos start beating the shit out of the Barbie-loving boy, and someone starts taking pictures, and a cop runs over, and then another, and any second the crowd is gonna yank bricks out of the wall and stone me to death because I don't know how to pilot a fucking sleigh across the moon, and finally the sixteen-year-old Santa Claus manager runs up and puts the 'Santa is out to Feed the Reindeer' sign up and tells me to get my ass in the office and the whole crowd, and there's like two hundred people now, starts booing me, and someone throws a chili dog at me, and I get to the office and the manager, he's a kid, okay? He's got a pimple the size of a grape on his forehead, okay, and his Elementary Algebra homework from third period on his desk!!! This future high school drop-out looks down his nose at me like I am a shit stain on society's Technicolor rainbow. And he confiscates my beard and my cap and tells me I can look for my check in the mail.

(Silence.)

TERRY. *(Finally:)* That's it?

ALEX. You want more?!?!?

BUCK. This is bullshit, they can't do that kind of —

ALEX. Big deal, you know what I learned from all this?

TERRY. That Joan Crawford is alive and well and shoppin' at the Gap!!!

ALEX. That too. No, I learned —

TERRY. Hey, ya can't take this personally, I mean it's no big secret that you ain't exactly the most authentic Santa Claus that ever lived —

ALEX. Terry. They replaced me with the Hindu guy from the newsstand! The only two English words he knows are CIGARETTE and LOTTO!!! I'm sure he'll be a hundred fuckin' percent more authentic! Kids all over New York'll be askin' for Quick Picks and cartons of Marboroughs!!!

BUCK. Hey don't worry, there's still that job in the administrative office —

TERRY. — and about a thousand auditions coming up —

ALEX. Auditions, Terry?? Office what?! I, I, I can't even keep a job for a month, sit-sitting on my ass going HO-HO-HO, you think I'm ever gonna make it as some kinda, some uh, executive in a polka-dot tie, or, or as some God-damned movie star?! Huh, Terry? Buck?!?! *(ALEX collapses in a chair, close to some kind of break-*

down.) I mean .... I just mean .... all I mean —

TERRY. Well I know what you mean, and I know what you need too. Buck and I are in the process of getting smashed and what you need to do is join Mommie and Christina!

(He goes into the kitchen.)

ALEX. *(The moment TERRY is out of the room:)* Buck ...
BUCK. *(Sits next to him:)* What, what, are you okay?
ALEX. I'm a total disaster. Look, I need to talk to you —

(TERRY bursts back in, a bottle and a glass:)

TERRY. Just found half a bottle of rum behind the Captain Crunch —
ALEX. Terry.
TERRY. Yes?
ALEX. Go to your room.
TERRY. Go to my what?
ALEX. Terry, please, for once, just this one time in all of our lives, you don't need a bitchy remark or a great exit line, just go to your room and let me finish talking to Buck, please, okay —
TERRY. But —
ALEX. — shh!
TERRY. — I —
ALEX. Terry, do it, I'm gonna get an elephant gun and fill it up with tranquilizer juice and blow you out the window, I need one minute, one second, I don't think I'm asking for a lot, Terry, I'm not asking for a lot here, do you think I'm asking for a lot?!?
TERRY. Alex.
ALEX. Terry.
TERRY. Are you calling me an elephant?
ALEX. Get out!!!
TERRY. *(Stares at him:)* Well you don't have to treat me like I'm irrational.

(He exits into his room, slamming the door.)

BUCK. What was that all about?

ALEX. Shut up. Please, Buck, let me finish —

BUCK. Finish WHAT, Alex, it's finished! You made sure I knew that! What do you want, Alex? What. Do. YOU. Want.

(A tense moment. They stare at each other.)

ALEX. Funny, I used to know exactly what I wanted, but some-where, everything went out of control, some carnival, a Ferris wheel, I'm goin' round and round, everyone's emotions along for the ride. I can't do that any more. I need one stable thing in my life. Some foun-dation of something. Somewhere to start ... um ... over, I mean ... because I think I lost track of what it is that me and Matt were sup-posed to be. You can't just love someone and then cheat on 'em and still love 'em ... pretend you love 'em-

BUCK. A zillion people do it every day.

ALEX. *(He gets the wrapped box, hands it to BUCK:)* I got you this for, um, Christmas, it's not much, but —

BUCK. I think you need to take a few weeks to —

ALEX. *(Quickly:)* I think I want to move in with you.

(Silence. BUCK stares at him.)

BUCK. Just like that.

ALEX. Just like that.

BUCK. You're an idiot.

ALEX. Yep.

BUCK. Are you trying to drive me crazy?? Cause, seriously —

ALEX. I thought it was what you wanted.

BUCK. It is! It was! I just —

ALEX. Then — ?

BUCK. Then you need to get back on your little Ferris wheel and spin around about twenty million more times til you're sure!

ALEX. Okay.

BUCK. I'm serious!

ALEX. So am I. You're right.

BUCK. I can't, I mean I can't believe this.

(TERRY emerges from his room, rum in hand.)

TERRY. Well I can't believe I have to stay locked in that room until New Year!

ALEX. ..... sh, j — Christ, I can't — Buck, just will you —

BUCK. Terry get the fuck out of here!

TERRY. I'm not Rapunzel!

ALEX. *(Desperate, the end of his rope:)* This is important!

TERRY. My life is important!

ALEX. *(Something cracks inside him and he lets loose:)* Yeah, real important, Terry, out there climbin' mountains, curin' cancer, carvin' your name in the sky, shit — !

TERRY. *(Deadly:)* Let me tell you ONE thing, Alex —

ALEX. — what're you, plastered up against the wall in there, a glass glued to your ear, real important life Terry! Ya drop off the planet tomorrow and no one'll wonder why!

TERRY. And what are you? What are you that's so incredible?!

ALEX. At least I —

TERRY. — what ALEX, at least you WHAT!? Lie? Cheat? Sell out? Give up?!

BUCK. Terry. Enough.

TERRY. You're no better than me, Alex!

BUCK. Terry, get outa here, okay, go get on the phone and ask Santa to bring you a new liver!

TERRY. Wooooo, Buck, that's real good comin' from someone who swallows a six-pack a day —

ALEX. I'm warnin' you Terry —

TERRY. You're warning me? Don't WARN me! I'm warning YOU, YOU FUCKING ASSHOLE!!!!

(He rages toward ALEX.)

BUCK. *(Holds him back:)* Enough, it's enough, okay?!

TERRY. Is it enough, Alex?! Is it?!! Tell me cause I really wanna know! My life isn't important, I TRY, whaddo you do?!? ALEX?! What do you do?! Failure! LOSER! You're no one!! You're NOTHING AT ALL!!!!

(ALEX punches him. TERRY falls backward, tangles with the coffee table, and sprawls to the floor, table and all. Flowers, drinks, papers spill everywhere. TERRY doesn't stay down, although he probably should. He's right back up and ready to kick ass, but the room is spinning like a top. Meanwhile, right after the punch, no pause, the following dialogue:)

BUCK. *(To ALEX:)* What're you doing?!?
ALEX. — oh God, oh shit, I'm sorry Terry, Jesus —
BUCK. — what's wrong with you?!
ALEX. I didn't mean it, Terry, God —
TERRY. *(Lunging back up, psycho eyes:)* Yeah, Alex, yeah, well I mean it!!! I really, REALLY mean it!!!

(He charges toward Alex but is so disoriented and spinning that when Buck grabs to hold him back, he only resists for a moment, before collapsing in Buck's arms.)

BUCK. *(As he grabs TERRY:)* I said that's it! You wanna both spend Christmas in Bellvue?!
TERRY. Who the hell do you think you are?! Rocky Balboa?!
ALEX. I'm sorry, Terry, I'm —
TERRY. Sorry, my ass, I'm sorry in the dead of night when I set your bed on fire!
BUCK. It's over okay?! Leave him alone!
TERRY. Leave — what?! After he — don't defend him Buck, I swear to God —
ALEX. Let's get outa here Buck, just let him cool off —
TERRY. Yeah, get outa here, go eat pancakes and talk about how awful I am, talk about fallin' in love and leavin' Matt, and Buck, you just sit there and believe it, you just sit there and let him string you along and string you along until there's nothin' left but —

(A key turns in the front door. It opens. A suitcase is pushed inside. Then another. A very short pause. MATT enters. He holds a duffel bag and a bag of presents. He is covered in snow, but is all smiles. He stands in the open doorway, grinning at everyone.)

MATT. Merry Christmas!

(BLACKOUT)

END ACT ONE

ACT II

Scene 1

(Christmas Eve. Almost three a.m.

*The apartment is a complete and total wreck. Red and green stream-
ers hang torn, limp, here and there. A balloon or two. Bottles
everywhere: beer bottles, booze bottles, soda bottles. The air is
filled with lingering cigarette smoke. Popcorn is scattered all
over the carpet. A punch bowl is filled with empty paper cups and
one or two remaining shots of eggnog. Several decimated cheese
balls. Tinsel. Balls of wrapping paper. Bows. Ribbons. All in all,
your basic post-Christmas-party disaster. Music still plays on the
stereo.*

*AT RISE: BUCK is lounging on the sofa, filled with tension, a beer
dangling in his hand. TERRY stands by the front door, a frazzled
mess. He shouts to people outside. We hear their garbled re-
sponses amid laughter, horns beeping, and car engines starting
up.)*

TERRY. *(To unseen, departing guests:)* Get home safe guys,
what?! No. No, don't let her drive, she thinks she's on Saturn. She's
got one brain cell left, what?! ...Yeah, merry, merry, happy, happy,
may all your merry-happy days be merry-happy-merry-ugh.

*(He slams the door. Leans against it. Slowly, he turns his head
around and looks at the apartment. His eyes are something out of
a horror movie.)*

BUCK. They've been gone twenty minutes. Not that I care.
TERRY. Oh. My. God. Will you look at this place?!?! All we

need now is water and Shelly Winters and we got *The Poseidon Adventure*!!!!!

BUCK. — I mean it's snowin' pretty hard, but how long does it take to drop off a coupla drunks? You don't think somethin' happened, do you Terry?

TERRY. What?!

BUCK. Matt and Alex —

TERRY. *(Takes a big swig of something, goes to the stereo:)* Shhhhhhhhh! I have a surprise for you!

BUCK. His tour doesn't   TERRY. Shhhh!!! Surprise!!!!!
end till next year — you don't
just show up —

TERRY. *(He slaps a CD in the stereo:)* — he lives here, Buck. It's his bed you been sleepin in, shut up, I have a —

BUCK. — he knows? What, what, I mean —

TERRY. *(Satan incarnate:) SURRRRPRISSSE!!!!!!!!!*

(BUCK shuts up — stares at him blankly. TERRY pushes play. A big sultry torch song blares out of the stereo. TERRY begins to "perform" the song, which he has obviously spent much time rehearsing for BUCK. After the first verse of the song:)

BUCK. Terry, I'm really not in the mood for —

TERRY. *(The scream of an insane banshee:) SHUUUUUT UUUUUUUUUUUUUUUUUUUUUUUUUUUP!!!!!!!!!!!!!!!!!!!!!!!!!!*

(And then fueled by a belly full of vodka, he continues his grand performance as if he is the grandest diva ever to land on Broadway, whipping a long strand of garland off the tree for use as a boa, straddling the coffee table as if he is lying on top of a grand piano, and generally tormenting BUCK in every way he possibly can. The "number" ends with TERRY in BUCK's lap. BUCK dumps him promptly onto the floor.)

BUCK. Terry. You really need to give therapy some serious thought.

TERRY. Yeah, if I'm crazy, Buck, and I probably am, I was

driven there by you and Alex. Matthew knows nothing! He's the last innocent guy in New York. He got a few days off and decided to surprise his boyfriend. No big plot. No psychedelic espionage. Just Merry Christmas! Get it? *We're* the bad guys, not him! This whole situation —

BUCK. — was YOUR idea!

TERRY. Wrong.

BUCK. You didn't beg us to please NOT tell Matt til after Christmas? You didn't say "Hey, let's just explain it for now by saying Buck and Terry are boyfriends." You didn't say that? Really brilliant, ya know. "Hi, Matt, what are you doing home? I'd like you to meet my new boyfriend, Buck."

TERRY. What can I tell ya, I always wanted to live out an episode of "Three's Company."

BUCK. Yeah, well, I never knew you were such a good actor.

TERRY. Just call me Joyce DeWitt, baby.

BUCK. What is this, method acting, something like that?

TERRY. What?!

BUCK. I'm just wondering, cause if you try to stick your tongue down my throat one more time, I'm gonna bite it off.

TERRY. *(Hitting him with a pillow from the couch:)* Oh that's great, I keep forgetting the level of maturity we're dealing with here!!!!!!

BUCK. After Christmas, he goes back on tour. His layover ends in a couple of days, he'll be gone, and Alex can send him a letter.

TERRY. We're all gonna burn in Hell.

BUCK. He won't blame you —

TERRY. Why wouldn't he? I got blame gushing out my asshole, pal! I been living right here in the same apartment as Alex —

BUCK. Alex ... won't be living here much longer.

TERRY. Yes he will, the lease doesn't end until April.

BUCK. Alex is moving in with me.

TERRY. Ahhhhh, no he's not.

BUCK. Yes he is, Terry, right after Matt leaves.

(The front door opens and MATT and ALEX enter, covered in snow.)

MATT. — you shoulda seen the room I was in Friday night —

ALEX. — cut it out, you're lying —

MATT. The Blue Moon Motor Lodge, that was the name. There's actually a place in America called the Blue Moon Motor Lodge.

(They both barrel over each other, laughing.)

TERRY. Sounds fancy.

MATT. It was fancy all right, we had fifteen fancy bullet holes in the wall —

TERRY. What?!

MATT. You could see right into the next room.

ALEX. What kinda tour is this? I don't want you in places like that!

MATT. That wasn't even the worst, wait. I pull down the bedspread, and the sheets are covered, I mean COVERED in dried blood.

TERRY. Oh my God!

MATT. Right? I mean I guess it's sort of fitting, appropriate, right? It's not like this is the national tour of friggin' *Phantom* or somethin'. No, I finally get a national tour of a show and they stick me in the vampire kick-line of *Salem's Lot, The Musical!*

TERRY. Don't complain, at least it's work.

MATT. Yeah, well I can guarantee you the cast of *Phantom* don't spend their nights holed up in the Blue Moon Motor Lodge wait'n for the serial killer to break down the door, no, no, no, they are off at the Hyatt Regency somewhere, eatin' grapes and vitamin balls and asparagus stalks, and gettin' suntans in little radiation beds while the beds in OUR hotels are where hookers come to DIE!

BUCK. So you guys got a little surprise vacation outa the deal, looks like —

MATT. Wichita, Kansas got cancelled, I think the advance sales were eighty-eight cents.

TERRY. What, no one wants to see singin' vampires on Christmas Eve?

MATT. This show's gonna kill me, and for what? Look at me. I weigh five pounds! This show's gonna kill me. We spend half of act two leapin on a giant neon cross that drips blood and then bursts into flames! I mean, what are we doing? This isn't what I dreamed of when I was a kid, watchin awards shows til one in the morning. I thought I'd play important parts ... say important things ... instead I close Act One screechin' a ballad called "Garlic".

TERRY. Well, we're all still waitin' for the happy ending I guess.

MATT. *(To ALEX:)* I got my happy ending right here.

ALEX. Hmmh ...

MATT. You're so quiet, cutie.

ALEX. Tired, ya know, Christmas, the whole —

BUCK. *(A little too firmly:)* So when do you go back?

MATT. Huh?

BUCK. To your little travelling circus or whatever —

TERRY. *(Plops down and wraps his arms around BUCK:)* Cutie, don't be weird!!!!!!!!!!!!!!!

ALEX. *(Gets up, heads to the bathroom:)* Excuse me.

MATT. Where did you guys meet each other, I mean —

TERRY. Well it was the funniest thing, we were both in this bar watchin reruns of "Three's Company" —

(ALEX exits into the bathroom, slamming the door a little too hard.)

MATT. *(To TERRY:)* Huh, did, I, uh, do something?

BUCK. So coupla days you were sayin?

MATT. What? Yeah, yeah the, we have to be in Seattle right after Christmas. *(About ALEX:)* What's wrong with him?

(ALEX flies out of the bathroom.)

ALEX. I need a drink. Anyone? Terry?

TERRY. Mix em strong, pleasssssse.

(Alex goes to the kitchen for drinks.)

BUCK. You know, you don't look anything like your picture.

MATT. Picture?

BUCK. The one in Alex's room. By the bed.

TERRY. *(To BUCK:)* You are just so kissable right now!
MATT. *(Going to kitchen, after ALEX:)* Back in a second.

(MATT exits.)

TERRY. *(Hits BUCK with a big pillow:)* The one by the bed!?
Who the hell do you think you are? Alexis Carrington?
BUCK. He's a fucking little pipsqueak. Here's what I was wor-
ried about?
TERRY. *(A warning:)* Hey.
ALEX. *(From the kitchen:)* No vodka, Terry.
TERRY. I'll take anything with a proof!
BUCK. He looks like a ten year old-weasel.
TERRY. Keep your jealous eighth grade bullshit to yourself, you
got what you wanted —
BUCK. I'm gonna tell him —
TERRY. Any decade Alex!
ALEX. *(From kitchen:)* They sucked down everything!
BUCK. He needs to know. It ends right here.
TERRY. Stop it! Stop it! STOP IT!!!!!!!! *(An idea:)* That's it,
I'm drinkin' backwash.

(And he does. ALEX enters, followed by MATT.)

ALEX. Skim milk and vermouth, that's it —
TERRY. *(Grabs the vermouth:)* Sold!
BUCK. Matt, come here, I wanna talk to you.
ALEX. What's going on.
TERRY. *(Chugs vermouth and backwash:)* How bout an encore
number?
BUCK. Shut up, I have something to say.
ALEX. What are you doing?

(TERRY turns the stereo on, loud. It's the same song as before.)

BUCK. Terry turn that shit off!
TERRY. Forget it, this is a desperate moment and it's screamin'

for a desperate measure!
    ALEX. It's three in the morning!

(BUCK is trying to turn off the stereo. TERRY is rummaging under the Christmas tree. BUCK pushes the wrong button. The sound blasts louder.)

MATT. *(Shouting over the music:)* What's wrong with you guys?! Everyone's acting like —

(Snap. BUCK turns off the music. At that exact moment, TERRY pulls a bottle-shaped gift from under the tree.)

TERRY. Alex and Buck, this was for you, but I am afraid I am going to have to commandeer the motherfucker —
    ALEX. Ummmm .....
    TERRY. Don't worry, I'll buy you a Mercedes tomorrow —
    MATT. Alex and Buck...?
    TERRY. *(Rips the paper off, revealing a bottle of something.)* Merry Christmas! Happy New Year! See ya later, boys, I'm leaving Las Vegas!

(He pops the lid and pours a huge shot into his mouth.)

MATT. Alex and Buck, you said —
    TERRY. *(Jumps on a table:)* Shots for everyone!
    ALEX. Terry, the neighbors — !

(MATT has picked through the bottle's wrapping paper. There was a card attached. He has grabbed it and now stands reading it.)

TERRY. Fuck the neighbors and fuck you too! *(SCREAMS WILDLY:)* W A K E   U P   M O T H E R F U C K -
ERS!!
    ALEX. Terry!!
    TERRY. SANTA CLAUS IS COMING TO TOWN AND HE'S PACKIN' HEAT!!!

(Instantly, there is banging on the wall from the apartment next door. Muffled shouts, etc. TERRY does not wait for the banging to stop. He responds like lightning.)

TERRY. UP YER ASS, BITCHBAG!!! THE GRINCH STOLE CHRISTMAS! FROSTY'S A PUDDLE OF MUD!!!

ALEX. ...T, wha, Terry, TERRY, shut your mouth, okay, TERRY! It's not funny —

MATT. "To Alex and Buck." That's what this card says.

ALEX. *(To TERRY:)* Get off the table!

MATT. Terry, you and Buck are going out, is that it?

TERRY. *(Quieter now:)* The Grinch stole Christmas ...

MATT. — cause I mean, that's what you told me, you all told me, so I just wanted to make sure I understood the situation —

ALEX. There's no situation —

MATT. Really, Alex? Mmmm, that's uh, good to know. So Buck, let me ask you, then ... are you going out with Terry?

TERRY. Maybe we should —

BUCK. What do you think.

MATT. I think I want an answer, are you dating? Are you kissing? Are you fucking?

BUCK. I gotta go home.

MATT. Why don't you do that. No one needs you here —

ALEX. Stop it.

MATT. Excuse me, what?

ALEX. Stop it Matt, you don't understand.

MATT. No, actually, I don't understand, Alex, but thanks, I think that might be the first honest thing you've said all night.

BUCK. I'm outa here —

MATT. You haven't returned my phone calls in three months, Al, is this why? Am I an idiot?! *(To BUCK:)* Someone like YOU would never even date someone like you *(TERRY)*! *(Losing it:)* And, and you *(ALEX)* have not been able to look me in the eye one time since I've been here.

TERRY. He would date me. He could date me ... *(To himself:)* ... he should date me.

ALEX. Terry get off the table before you break your skull.
TERRY. *(Happy, bright:)* Maybe we should all go to bed now.
MATT. Shut up, Terry.

(MATT exits quickly into ALEX's bedroom.)

TERRY. *(More happiness:)* Sleep nice and late, wake up happy, drive over to my mother's for a big Christmas dinner —
ALEX. Your mother's dead, you killed her, remember?!?!?!
TERRY. *(Vicious:)* Well maybe we should all go to bed now anyway!!! BEFORE I SHED any MORE blood!!
MATT. *(Returning from bedroom with suitcases:)* Relax Terry, it's over, okay, but thanks for the card, it was really enlightening.

(MATT goes back into the bedroom.)

ALEX. *(To MATT:)* What are you doing? It's three in the —
MATT. *(Re-enters with the rest of his bags and a coat:)* "To Alex and Buck, Love Terry", and a very sweet sentiment on the inside of the card too. Let's see here. *(Reads:)* "Merry Christmas to my favorite adulterer and mistress." Aw, some holiday humor. You always were the campy one. But wait, there's more. "Have fun in the new year living in sin. Love, Terry." *(He pauses for one deadly moment:)* I really don't think I should be here right now. For your sake and mine.
ALEX. Matt —
BUCK. Don't worry, I'm leaving.
MATT. *(About to lose it:)* You keep sayin' that but you haven't moved! Go on, hit the road! Maybe Santa'll drop you off a couple of alphabet books!
BUCK. Wait a minute, if you got a problem with —
MATT. — I got a problem all right, can ya guess what it is?
BUCK. I wouldn't waste the energy.
MATT. Well waste a little walkin' out the front door before someone has to call 911—
TERRY. Alrighty then.
MATT. — if you can handle Alex sleeping with his lover for one night instead of you!

ALEX. You're assuming things you know nothing about!

MATT. Assume?! Assume nothing Alex, you're a real good actor over the phone on your one call every three months, with the static blazin' from five hundred miles away, but in person, with the spotlight on you, the whole thing's melting all over your face! Assume?!? Fuck assume! Admit it! Right now! Just stand here and look at me and say the words!

(A short but tense moment. BUCK grabs his coat and bolts toward the front door.)

ALEX. *(Grabs him:)* Buck —

BUCK. I'll wait in the car for five minutes. Then I'm leaving. For good.

(SLAM. He is gone. ALEX whirls on MATT, furious.)

ALEX. You don't know what's goin' on.
MATT. I can figure —
ALEX. You have no idea!

(He turns to go. Opens the front door.)

MATT. *(Quickly, full of rage and fire and devastation:)* If you go after him right now instead of standing here and facing me with the truth — ! *(SLAM. He leaves. MATT stares in total and complete disbelief.)* Oh. Wow. He … he left. Did you, uh, see that, Terry?

TERRY. Matthew … men are pigs okay? That's all there is, one fact you need to know in life to get by.

MATT. What just happened, I don't know what just happened here —

TERRY. Pigs, okay, they have this, this pig gene, I never wanna see another man again, I'm gonna go join that militant Christian group that brainwashes you into being straight in a three-week bible class! I'm gonna take my new improved heterosexual self and meet up with Miss America somewhere, take her off to Kansas, pop out three screeching brats, and sit around in my underwear in my backyard by the grill and suck down six packs of Old Milwaukee for the rest of my life, fantasizing about tits, and puss, and the Super Bowl!!! *(Matt has found the wrapped gift ALEX gave to BUCK at the end of Act One. As TERRY finishes his speech, MATT swipes it from underneath the tree.)* — What are you doing?

MATT. This says "TO BUCK". Is it from you?

TERRY. *(A terrified lie:)* ... yes ...

MATT. What is it?

TERRY. ... socks.

MATT. *(Pulling violently at the ribbons:)* You people need to get your God-damned shit together, try to pull off some big plot, leave evidence lyin' all over the place, do you think I'm that STUPID?!

TERRY. Fine, Miss Marple, you cracked the case! What can I say!

MATT. Who is this from?! Is this from Alex?!

TERRY. How the hell do I know who it's from! What are you doing?!

MATT. What do you think I'm doing?!

TERRY. *(Hysterical, grabs it:)* NO! Are you nuts?! You wanna make things worse?!

MATT. *(Grabs it back:)* Things couldn't get any worse!

TERRY. *(Holds onto the gift for dear life, and as MATT walks off with it, TERRY drags behind.)* Sure they could, things can always get worse, just when you think —

MATT. — Terry! —

TERRY. — couldn't get any worse, the living room blows up! The Student Loan companies track you down. Your ex-lover flies into the room and tears your head off! .

(MATT releases the gift. TERRY, who had been pulling on it, slams onto the floor. The box tumbles beside him.)

MATT. Ex?

TERRY. What?!

MATT. Ex-lover! You said EX!

TERRY. Hypo — what? Matt, I'm too drunk for this — Hypothetically, I just meant hypoth, the living room's not really gonna blow up, Jesus —

MATT. He's not my ex-lover, Terry.

TERRY. And all the student loan companies'll find when they track me down is the smoke around my tombstone.

MATT. He's not my —

TERRY. Not your ex, not your ex, fine, great, you're Lucy and Ricky, you're Fred and Wilma, you're whatever you wanna be, now just back off! I can't tell if you're gonna knife me or sing a torch song!

MATT. *(Advancing on TERRY:)* Terry give me that box.

TERRY. *(Backs away:)* Get your own box.

MATT. What the hell is in there, Terry?!

TERRY. Jimmy Hoffa and Amelia Earhart, locked in embrace!

MATT. Who do you think you're protecting?!

TERRY. You, Matt! I'm protecting you! And I'm protecting ME!!! Because whatever's in that box is gonna send you into a panic attack and I can't take any more panic attacks in this apartment! I went through this whole lousy fuck of a year and I finally made it to Christmas, and in a week, I get a brand new chance to start from scratch and see if I can fuck my life up even bigger than it already is! It's Christmas and I made it and what's my reward?! Diamonds? A ham?! NO!!! I get emergency at every doorstep! Everyone I know has turned into Lady Macbeth and I can't take it any more, so fine! Let's go! Out damned spot, let's rip 'er open! *(He grabs the box, starts tearing it open.)* Don't just stand there! Come on get into it! Break something! *(He has torn the box open to reveal a big fluffy teddy bear.)* Well, whadaya know, it's the invasion of Winnie the Pooh!!! *(Quieter now:)* You happy now Matt? You know what you wanted to know? Is this your ideal Christmas Eve or what?!

MATT. *(Wiped out, emotionless:)* Oh wow.

TERRY. *(Sucks down some more liquor. Then:)* You got some real nerve flyin' in here, causin' all the, rallin' all the, frallin' a, a ... huh?

MATT. *(Soft, serious:)* I think maybe things are really messed up here right now.

TERRY. Fruggin' right, *(Drinks more:)* all this mess for a stuffed bear, prob'ly cost fifty cents Times Sware. Square.

MATT. I don't know what to do.

TERRY. Who cares what you do, just throw the God-damned thing out the window, that stupid teddy bear lovin motherfucker.

MATT. Yeah. Yeah. Mmm. Phhu.

(He opens a window and hurls the bear out into the night.)

TERRY. Holy shit whaddid ya just do?!?

MATT. I threw it out the window.

TERRY. Whaddid ya DO?! I mean jus — whhoah — whaddid ya — this woom, I'm onna merry go round! I'm havin' bed spins! Where's the bed?!

MATT. Terry would you please just shut up!!!

TERRY. *(Advances on MATT, waving the bottle wildly:)* You know, I've had just about enough a you people tellin' ol' Terry ta shut up alla time. Ol' Terry's had just about enough!

MATT. Sit down! You're drunk!

TERRY. Ol' drunk Terry! Out the window! Out damned spot! Throw it all away! *(MATT turns away.)* Hey! *(TERRY pushes him in the back so hard he almost knocks him down. MATT whirls around, furious.)* Maybe — maybe nobody ever loved me Matt ...... but at least I don't have an ex-lover! *(MATT shoves him, not very hard, but it doesn't take much. TERRY stumbles into the coffee table, spilling things everywhere. Somehow, he keeps his balance.)* Oh yeah? Ohh really? Jus push me, huh? I'm some kinda pushover, huh? Lemme tell you somethin' Matt. I jus wanna tell you somethin' Matt! I jus wanna tell you this one. Tiny. Fact!

(He raises the bottle like it's some kind of mini baseball bat and then swings it at MATT, who easily avoids being bashed in the head by stepping calmly aside. TERRY, led by the bottle, swings around in a complete circle and smacks into the Christmas tree, which crashes to the ground, TERRY in tow.)

MATT. Terry are you out of your mind?!?

TERRY. *(From somewhere under the tree:)* I jus ... wanted to .... knock some sense in to somebody.

(And with that, he passes out cold. At that instant, the front door flies open. ALEX stands in the doorway holding the now muddy, teddy bear.)

ALEX. *(Soft, angry:)* What is this.
MATT. I'd ask you the same thing.
ALEX. What do you think you're doing.
MATT. Trying to figure out —
ALEX. He's important to me!!!

(ALEX hurls the bear at MATT and slams the door with all his might. Instantly he bursts into heaving, sobbing tears, collapsing against the door, sliding down it into a crouching position on the floor. MATT is totally stunned.)

MATT. W ... wait a, just a second here. You're crying? Huh? You're crying over this, over HIM?!
ALEX. You don't know —
MATT. Alex... Alex, what did you do, go and fall in love with him?
ALEX. Just leave, go back to —
MATT. Did you?!?
ALEX. *(A very long pause, then, softly:)* I love him.
MATT. .... Oh .... oh .... huh, that shut me right up, didn't it. Unless maybe I heard you wrong. Maybe I heard you wrong?
ALEX. I love him, Matt.
MATT. Oookay, that's two for two, I guess, um, ... wow, boy, suddenly I feel really stupid, because, what, three, four days ago on the phone, when I actually got through to you for five minutes, you were sayin' you loved me!
ALEX. I do love you.
MATT. Bullshit, how is that possible?!? How can you love two people at once?! No one has that much love to go around!
ALEX. I didn't look for this. It happened.
MATT. You let it happen!
ALEX. I didn't want to hurt you.

MATT. I will not hold a conversation in Barry Manilow song lyrics!!! You tell me something I haven't heard a hundred times or don't tell me anything!

ALEX. Just ... go back to your tour.

MATT. No. I love you Alex. Why won't you look at me, you gotta have some kind of feeling after all the time we were together, what, what, um, happened, I mean, to forever? Forever, forever, that's all you ever said — !

ALEX. That doesn't exist. It's just some word from fairy tales.

MATT. We had something good.

ALEX. I know.

MATT. We were good for each other.

ALEX. Matt —

MATT. We still are, just forget it, mistakes, we all, okay ... forget this ever happened. I've been gone a long time, I can try to understand —

ALEX. You're leaving again.

MATT. I don't have to —

ALEX. It's your career.

MATT. I'll drive a cab, I'll sweep a floor. You're what matters to me.

ALEX. It's over, Matt.

MATT. Look at me.

ALEX. I have to go.

MATT. Look me in the eye one time! You owe me that much!

ALEX. *(Stares at the floor:)* ... I can't.

MATT. Then stay. Please, Alex, stay with me one night, tonight, maybe we can, I mean, after all we had —

ALEX. I know..... I know, Matt. We had .... *(He can't finish.)* ... It's too late, okay? I take the blame, all of it, I'm the asshole, the bad guy, the jerk. I could've stopped this. I could've tried harder. I didn't. I got lonely. Simple as that. And I wasn't strong enough ... to turn away ... when some one wanted to hold me.... I should've stopped it. I didn't. I fell in love with him. And if you can believe this, Matt ... I love you too.... But too much has happened ... and I can't remember ... I just, I can't remember the way it was. With you. With us. I love you Matt ... but I don't think I'm in love with you any more.

(ALEX looks at MATT in the eye for the first — and maybe last — time. A horn beeps outside. They keep staring at each other. MATT walks toward ALEX slowly, very slowly. He reaches him, stares at him. Then wraps his arms around him. They embrace. Silently. Honestly. Finally, ALEX pulls away. He seems embarrassed, confused, and breaks eye contact sharply. He pauses for a moment, and then goes quickly to the front door. He exits, leaving the door wide open. MATT stares after him and, as a car is heard driving away into the night, he exits into the bedroom, shutting the door softly behind him.
Silence.
Then, the Christmas tree rustles.)

TERRY. *(Completely wasted out of his mind:)* ..... hey ......
hey! .... I'm trapped! .... *(Bette Midler, "The Rose":)* ... where are
you goin'?.... where are you goin' where's everybody goin'?

(He cracks up, cackling at his own lousy impression. As he laughs like a lunatic, tangled under the tree, ROGER comes to the entrance of the front door. Knocks. Looks in.)

ROGER. Hello?
TERRY. *(From under the tree:)* Jesus, is that you?
ROGER. Anyone home?
TERRY. I'm home Jesus, Sweet baby Jesus I'm home, come fly
your tragic sister up to paradise!

(TERRY emerges from below the tree, covered in tinsel and garland and pine needles, an ornament stuck in his hair, a bow stuck on his face, and a popcorn string tangled on his ear. He is, as usual, a complete wreck.)

ROGER. Wow man, what's goin' on in here? You guys have a
party or somethin'?
TERRY. *(Confused, disoriented:)* Wha ..?!
ROGER. Howya doin', what's your name again? Steve? José?
TERRY. *(Thinks about it, then:)* José.

ROGER. I was jus' walkin' home, saw your lights on, my aunt had this big Christmas party, it's still goin' on. Neighbors called the cops three times. Guess they didn't know the cops were already there, suckin' down eggnog with my Uncle Sal.

TERRY. I think I'm gonna be sick.

ROGER. You guys really tore this place up. Shit, I thought my party was wild but at least we didn't knock down the tree.

TERRY. I can't be sick, I'm never sick, I hold my lumber like a liquorjack.

ROGER. Me too, boy, we	TERRY. ....….................
got that in common, I musta	maybe I'll make a little exception
done like ten tequila shots	just this once! Oh God, okay, shh,
and that ain't even countin' —	SHHH!!! Lemme just concentrate
	a minute, um, okay. Okay.

ROGER. You okay?

TERRY. No. Happy thoughts, happy thoughts. Kittens, ummmmm, Disneyland, a million bucks, my own apartment —

ROGER. You're lookin' about fifteen different colors right now.

TERRY. Yeah? That usually happens right before split pea soup shoots outa your mouth.

ROGER. You want me to go?

TERRY. No. Ya think?

ROGER. Cause the door was open.

TERRY. So's the door at Denny's but that don't mean they want you to walk through it at four o'clock on Christmas morning! What the hell are you doing here!

ROGER. I told you, my aunt, she lives like four blocks away, down on —

TERRY. I gotta go to bed, I don't mean to be rude, but get the fuck out.

ROGER. Cause I was wonderin', you know, is that Buck guy around?

TERRY. No, Roger Ramone, that Buck guy is definitely not around —

ROGER. He was pretty hot.

TERRY. I gotta siddown, I gotta lie down, I gotta just uh — *(He collapses on the sofa; a rag doll:)* Yeah. There. Okay ... I might be okay now.

ROGER. So … you sure you want me to go?

TERRY. I'm seein' like four of you right now, this couch feels like the Tilt-A-Whirl, I don't know how my tongue is forming these words, the only thing I know for sure is I want you to go!!!

ROGER. You don't like me anymore?

TERRY. You only like ME when someone better looking's not around.

ROGER. *(Moving in for the kill:)* I think you're about as hot as they come.

TERRY. This isn't happening.

ROGER. It's true.

TERRY. Great, great, m-j — mail me a post card, huh, this —

ROGER. *(Sitting next to him:)* How 'bout I just hold you a few minutes.

TERRY. How bout maybe not, huh?

(But ROGER does hold him … and it feels good.)

TERRY. Um, I can't do this right now, you appeared out of no-where like Elizabeth Montgomery —

ROGER. *(Rocking him:)* — shhhhhhh ....

TERRY. You're a hallucination. I'm outa control —

ROGER. I like guys outa control.

TERRY. Well I am. My life, everything. I can't live like this any-more, I just need —

ROGER. Shhh ...

TERRY. I just need something. One thing. If I had one thing —

ROGER. Relax, just —

TERRY. Even people I don't know tell me to relax, what can this mean?

ROGER. It means you're a fuckin' ball of nerves, even when you're trashed.

TERRY. I guess if two liters of vodka doesn't work, nothing will.

ROGER. Never say nothing.

(He kisses TERRY. Strong. Deep. Brimming with rough passion.

Then , at once, he stops. Brushes the tinsel out of TERRY's hair.)

TERRY. ... what, ahhh, what was —
ROGER. Still want me to go?
TERRY. I just want ... I just want .... everyone I know's in love with everyone else I know. And no one's ever been in love with me. Ever. I just wanna know what that feels like.
ROGER. I can show you. *(Kisses him.)*
TERRY. ... someone to love me ...
ROGER. Mmmm ... *(Kisses his neck.)*
TERRY. Just ... one ... time ...
ROGER. *(His voice is full of raw lust. He can't contain it:)* Let's go to your room.
TERRY. I can't do anything.
ROGER. *(Helping him up:)* I'll do everything.
TERRY. I don't do anything. Nothing's safe.
ROGER. I got condoms. Come on.

(He is walking TERRY, practically carrying him, toward the hall.)

TERRY. I don't do anything, just roll around a little, must be boring. No one ever calls me after I've had sex with 'em once ... not even sex. Just rolling around.
ROGER. Which one's your room?

(TERRY makes a limp motion toward one of the doors.)

TERRY. My name's not José.
ROGER. Okay.

(ROGER keeps walking him toward the door.)

TERRY. Just for future reference.
ROGER. Whatever you say, man.
TERRY. Roger?
ROGER. Mmmm.
TERRY. Has anyone ever been in love with you?

ROGER. *(He pauses; looks at TERRY:)* Love? Shit. I got more fuckin' love 'n I know what to do with.

(They are in the doorway of TERRY's room now.)

TERRY. Yeah? Who you got that loves you so much, Roger Ramone? Your teddy bear? Your goldfish?... Your boyfriend?
ROGER. My wife.

(Before TERRY can even attempt to react, ROGER spins him into the bedroom. Slam. They are gone.)

(Quick BLACKOUT)

Scene 2

(The next morning. Christmas morning.
Well, not morning actually. Actually closer to twelve noon, but all our major characters are still passed out, so we'll just call it morning. The apartment is exactly how we left it, the only difference being that now, bright late morning sunshine is blazing in the window, making the party disaster area seem even more hopeless than before.
A beat.
The door to TERRY's room flies open and ROGER rushes out, with TERRY trailing close behind. Instant pandemonium. ROGER's shirt is open. His hair is in every direction. He is buttoning his pants and searches wildly for his shoes during the following. Terry is in some insane state of semi-undress, and as always, is an utter and complete wreck.)

ROGER. *(Immediate, upon entering:)* — outa my mind, must be outa my mind —
TERRY. — look jus' relax and —

ROGER. — shoes, my fucking shoes, where — ?!

TERRY. — siddown, jus —

ROGER. — outa my mind, I'm dead! You understand that? I'm DEAD!

TERRY. — shh, okay, shhh —

ROGER. — shoes, just help me —!

TERRY. Shoes, great, uh —

ROGER. What was I thinkin', huh? Christmas, Christmas fuckin' mornin' and I'm —

TERRY. *(Finds a shoe:)* — here —

ROGER. I got a wife, a baby girl waitin'! What am I doin' here?!?

TERRY. Quit screaming at me! My skull's gonna shatter! How am I supposed to know what you're doin' here?! I swallowed a liquor store last night! Finding your naked ass sprawled all over my bed was as much a surprise to me, OKAY?!?

ROGER. I wasn't supposed to sleep with you. I got obligations!

TERRY. Well, whad the hell I do, dump Unisom down your throat?!?

ROGER. Shit, let me think, just lemme sit, I gotta think I gotta — on fuckin' Christmas I do this shit! I didn't even finish puttin' the tricycle together! Fuck me! Fuck! Shit!

TERRY. I've had complaints after sex, but this is ridiculous.

ROGER. SEX?!? What sex?!? You call that sex?!?

TERRY. We had our clothes off. We bounced around a little.

ROGER. Bounced around?! You took one lick on my nipple and passed out cold!

TERRY. Well what do you want from me in the middle of the nineties, that I should be a God-damned sperm depository or somethin'?!?

ROGER. NO!! But you could at least be conscious!

TERRY. Details.

ROGER. For this my life is ruined?! For this I'm gonna get the Christmas turkey hurled at my head the second I walk through the front door?!

TERRY. Hey, look, you came to me! What do you think you're doin', whorin' around with guys when you got a family?! If I knew

that —
    ROGER. Don't fuckin' judge me — !
    TERRY. I'm just sayin — !
    ROGER. You don't know what I go through —
    TERRY. You don't know what I go through! No wonder I'm
slidin' toward my thirties and still alone when these are the pickins
that are out there! I just went to bed with a married with children psy-
cho-slut who doesn't care what he's fucking as long as it has a
pulse!!!
    ROGER. Nice.
    TERRY. It's not true?!
    ROGER. Who cares, I gotta go —
    TERRY. Great idea, this whole thing's makin' me sicker by the
minute —
    ROGER. Yeah? Well, you're no fuckin' prize yourself, kid.
    TERRY. Who said I was?
    ROGER. Just cause you think the world's one big asshole, but
your shit smells like orange blossoms.
    TERRY. Yeah?
    ROGER. Just to let you know, it doesn't.
    TERRY. Doesn't?
    ROGER. Smell like orange blossoms.... It's more like eighty
proof.

*(MATT enters from the bedroom. His hair is wild. His eyes, bloodshot
    and lifeless. Night clothes. He stands in the doorway like a bro-
    ken toy.)*

    TERRY. *(In response to ROGER's jab:)* Ooooh, ya been workin'
on that one all night?
    ROGER. Happy New Year, Steve.

*(He smiles smugly, grabs his coat and exits. MATT and TERRY stand
    silently for a moment.)*

    MATT. Where'd he come from.
    TERRY. Santa Claus dropped him off.

MATT. Mmm.

TERRY. He didn't fit. I had to send him back.

MATT. Who's Steve?

TERRY. Prob'ly the guy he fucked before me.

MATT. Sheer class.

TERRY. Well. Merry Christmas anyway.

MATT. Huh. Well, get ready for your Christmas present.

TERRY. I got a present?

MATT. You got fired.

TERRY. Fired?

MATT. From your job. They called. You're fired. Merry Christmas.

TERRY. I'm not fired.

MATT. Mmm.

TERRY. I'm not fired, I'm not, what he hell are you talking about, they adore me there! I'm submissive, subservient, I cower to authority, everything restaurant managers love!

MATT. Your mother thought you were working this morning.

TERRY. She didn't call the restaurant. I told her not to call the restaurant.

MATT. She wanted to say Merry Christmas. The waitress who answered the phone thought she was calling from beyond the grave and passed out cold in a Western omelet.

TERRY. WHAT?!

MATT. They had to call the paramedics and everything. She burned both her eyebrows off in the hash browns.

TERRY. I told her not to call me at work! I told her not to call me — !

MATT. She called twice. She called back, after, you know getting disconnected, and this time, the owner answered —

TERRY. This is nuts! Now what do I do?!

MATT. Leave town. Your boss wants a hundred and sixty-nine dollars and ninety-five cents by Monday.

TERRY. What?!?

MATT. For the flowers.

TERRY. Godohgodohgod —

MATT. Or he says you're gonna need flowers for real.

TERRY. I knew I never should've worked for a Mafia owned diner.

MATT. I knew I never should've gone on this tour.

TERRY. I just don't think people are supposed to get fired on Christmas Day, isn't, isn't that like against the law?

MATT. It's against the law to get dumped on Christmas Eve, I know that.

TERRY. *(Genuine empathy:)* Aw, Matt ...

MATT. No, no, it's fine.

TERRY. It's not fine.

MATT. Terry, I'm just saying, do I look upset about this?

TERRY. You look like road kill, and I'm sorry, but if your eyes were any more bloodshot, I'd whip out my garlic and crucifix.

MATT. *(A deep guttural sigh:)* Uhhhhhhhggghhhhhhhhhhh.

TERRY. I just ... Matt. I just need you to understand.... Maybe this isn't the right time for, uh, for me to um, but —

MATT. Terry, please.

TERRY. I just don't want you to be mad at me.

MATT. You're supposed to be my friend!

TERRY. You're supposed to be MY friend and understand that this was nothing I could stop!

MATT. As if you tried — !

TERRY. I DID TRY! I bitched! I screamed! I nagged Alex to the point where he can't stand the sight of me anymore, what else was I supposed to do?!? Take him to the vet and have him neutered?!

MATT. No, Terry, no, I just wanted to know this was going on!!! One phone call! One tip off!

TERRY. A TIP OFF?! I'm sorry, what — a TIP OFF ?!? Now I'm Liz fucking Smith?!?

MATT. What's the matter with you?

TERRY. No job, no money, no liver.

MATT. This isn't a joke, Terry!

TERRY. Who said it was?! We got a Christmas tree that looks like it survived Hiroshima! WHO lives like this?! Bankers? Throw a coupla crack whores in the corner and we got ourselves a real nice happy ending, baby!

MATT. *(Collapses on the sofa, no emotion:)* I don't believe this.

TERRY. Well don't worry, the Grinch'll be by any second. His shitty little heart grows ten sizes too big and he brings Christmas back to all the happy Whos! *(Waits for a response. None.)* Happy, happy, happy! Merry, merry! *(No response.)* Well ... he better get his little green ass over here and bring back Christmas or it looks like I single-handedly destroyed two perfectly flawless marriages. After all, if only I'd remembered to keep Alex locked in the broom closet, you two'd be unwrapping little puppy dogs and chocolate angels right now.... And lets not forget the straight married FATHER who I RAPED last night! He didn't have time to put the tricycle together, ya know, cause after all, who can resist swingin from the chandelier with me?!... I think it's pretty clear how all of this is MY fault. Right, Matt?...Look ... listen.... I'm sorry, I really am, I wanted to call you ... look, um ... we can go to my mom's house, she's doin that big dinner, all five hundred relatives'll be there but at least it'll seem like a holiday ... Matt? Mashed potatoes?... Pumpkin pie?... Hey maybe she'll undercook the turkey again and we can watch the whole family get botulism!

(MATT suddenly bursts into tears. There are no words. TERRY goes to the sofa and holds him. A very quiet moment.)

MATT. *(Finally, a little embarrassed:)* I can't be here any more....
TERRY. Its okay....
MATT. *(Gets up quickly, pushing TERRY aside:)* No. Nothing is okay. Nothing.

(MATT starts fumbling recklessly around the apartment, collecting his belongings, shoving them into his suitcases, throwing on jeans, a sweatshirt, etc.)

TERRY. What are you doing?
MATT. I can't be here! All I hear is Alex telling me about forever.
TERRY. You can't plan that far!
MATT. I did! We did! If you can't plan for that what can you plan for?!

TERRY. You can't plan for anything, okay?! Everyone runs around in circles, planning this and planning that, and sometimes the plans work. And sometimes they crash. Sometimes the Grinch gives Christmas back to all the little Whoville couples, and sometimes he just lets them all rot in the ice. Happy endings must happen, Matt, I guess they do, somewhere ... all the movies say they do, but I haven't seen too much of that in real life. That doesn't mean we can't wake up on New Years Day and start all over again. Matt ... look ... there was, uh ... there was this day back in October. I went over to the mall after work .... to talk to Buck about this. About you. And Alex. The whole, um, thing had been goin on for a while and this was when you started to ask me all kinds of questions about why he wasn't returning your calls and I couldn't ...... didn't say anything — what was I gonna, um, so I go to the mall and they're havin this huge car show lined up from Sears to the J.C. Penny, and all these little displays too, like a booth to win a new Mercedes, and there was some computer race car thing, and a couple of booths about driving safely —

MATT. Terry what the hell are you talking about?

TERRY. I noticed all this crap cause I was walking really slow, you know, to Buck's office. What the hell was I doin there, anyway? I shouldn't be there, it's not my business, I should be out findin my own soap opera to star in, where I play the lead and I get the trauma and the drama and the long stem rose: ιn Valentines Day .... who am I to go in here and tell these boys to cease and desist. It's NONE OF MY BUSINESS. So, I'm walking really slow, through this car expo, ya know, thinkin about what to say, or should I just go home, and all of a sudden, I'm at this big gigantic exhibit right in the middle of the mall. It's a car, right, with two crash test dummies in the front seat. And its one of those things, like at a theme park, an audio, whatever, animatronical thing that moves. There's this wall, see, a fake wall, and the car is on this short little track. So these crash test dummies, they talk. They say, "Hiya folks! We're gonna show you how the Cougar XR-40 can save your life!" The next thing I know, the car goes flyin into this wall! The front of the car crumples up like an accordion and PA-POOFATAH! This big white airbag inflates in the front seat and saves the dummies from decapitation.

MATT. I don't know where you think you're goin with this.

TERRY. Goin for the metaphor, babe, stay with me.... So. So then the little animatronic guy says "Don't be a dummy. Drive safe." And the crowd applauds like if they just saw opening night of Star Wars. The airbag deflates, the car uncrumples, and the dummies do the same thing all over again. I stood there watchin it for like fifteen minutes. Crash! Crumple! Airbag! Poof! Like twenty times. This display musta cost a million dollars!

MATT. So what's your poignant little metaphor, Emily Dickenson? That life is just an endless car wreck?

TERRY. No.

MATT. Then what —

TERRY. You can get out of the car, dummy.

MATT. Yeah?

TERRY. Let the car crash without you. Get out of the car. Move on. Look its obvious, I'm not the fuckin Poet Laureate of Staten Island, okay? Uh, it's just you got a choice. We all do. We can sit in the car and get battered 'til our brains fall out, or we can get out before it hits the wall again. It's easy. It's obvious. Life isn't so obvious. Who gives a fuck? Just live and be happy, and try not to get to banged up along the way. Drive safe, babe. Don't be a dummy.

MATT. *(Laughs humorlessly:)* Jesus Christ. And did you talk to Buck? Or did you just watch the crash test all day?

TERRY. I talked to him.

MATT. And you told him —

TERRY. I asked him out.

MATT. You —

TERRY. — told him congratulations on his car expo, he's in charge of all that shit, and I asked him if he might wanna try goin out with someone single for a change .... and he said no, of course, what else was he gonna say, *(very softly:)* he had Alex's picture on his desk. *(MATT is silent for a long moment.)* Get outa the car, Matt. No more car wrecks til next year. *(TERRY gives MATT a big hug. Then they stare at each other a moment.)* You're gonna be fine. We all are.

(He goes to the sofa, sits down, flicks on the TV. The end of "How the Grinch Stole Christmas" is playing. Again MATT stands behind TERRY for a moment. The lights have started to fade, very, very

slowly.)

MATT. Maybe we could go to your mom's for dinner....

TERRY. — sure, of course, we can —

MATT. I just wanna lay down a little first, Terry. Can I use your room? I can't — I mean I can't —

TERRY. Sure, make, make yourself at home. Mine's the bed that smells like cheap sex and Absolut.

(MATT laughs a little, in spite of himself.)

TERRY. I hate the endings of Christmas specials.

MATT. Why?

TERRY. They're always .... huh .... well .... Merry Christmas, kiddo.

MATT. *(A pause. He smiles at TERRY:)* Merry Christmas.

(MATT exits into TERRY's room, shuts the door behind him. TERRY goes to the Christmas tree, which is still laying on the floor. He rights it and tries the lights. They still work. As he stands beside the tree, the star seems to grow just a little brighter.)

TERRY. .... Merry, merry Christmas.

(CURTAIN)

END OF PLAY

PROPERTIES LIST

FURNITURE:

Sofa
Chair
Coffee table
Smaller tables

PROPS:

Christmas tree
Christmas lights (practical)
Christmas ornaments
Christmas tinsel
Phone (practical ringer)
Television with VCR hook-up
Remote control (optional)
VCR
Tape: "How the Grinch Stole
    Christmas"
Answering machine (possibly
    practical)
Tape for answering machine
Bowl of popcorn
Microwave popcorn for run
2 strings of popcorn with needles
Wrapped box with Teddy bear
    with ring on ribbon — and
    tag
Unwrapped duplicate Teddy
    bear, muddy
Wrapping paper (lots for run)
Sticky bows (lots for run)
Ribbon (lots for run)

Christmas tags (lots for run)
Bag of wrapped gifts
2 suitcases with Matt's clothes
Duffel bag
Wrapped bottle of liquor with tag
Several funeral bouquets with cards
Half a bottle of rum
Clean glass
Snow for Terry, Roger, Buck,
    Alex and Matt's entrances
Large, full dance bag
2 glasses containing screwdrivers
Roger's business cards (a few for
    the run)
Lots of empty beer bottles
Lots of empty soda bottles
Lots of empty liquor bottles
2 full bottles of beer
Red and green streamers (lots for
    the run)
Balloons
Punch bowl, empty of eggnog
Paper party cups (lots for the run)
Briefcase for Buck (optional)
Bag for Alex (optional)
Instant ice tea to color the rum
Apartment dressing
Christmas dressing
Cheese balls
Cheese ball sculptures that are
    smashed every night
Cigarette butts and ashtrays
(optional)
Wrapped gifts for under the tree

SET PLAN

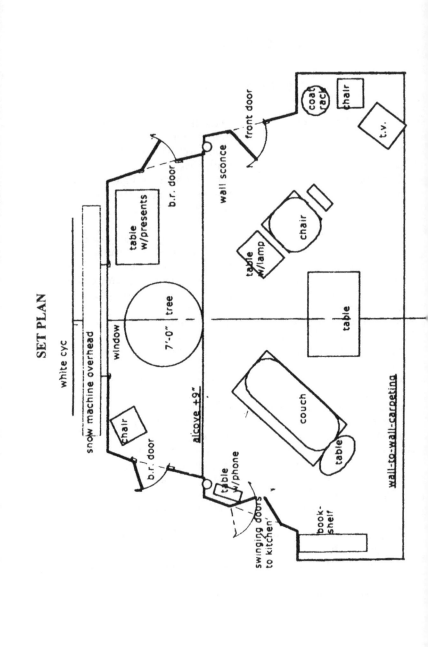